Three Hearts Entwined

Cauldron Falls, Volume 4

Solara Gordon

Published by THE EARTH MOVED, LLC, 2024.

THREE HEARTS ENTWINED

First edition. June 26, 2024.

Copyright © 2024 Solara Gordon.

ISBN: 979-8988654957

Written by Solara Gordon.

Who knew Cauldron Falls would ignite sparks of story after story? Certainly my readers did! They want and are asking for more! This one is for my readers, my readers group and street team: Solara's Glamorous Stars! You inspire me. You cheer me on. Provide story ideas and keep asking for more. A special thank you goes out to Chevy Allen for beta reading and catching blips. To all my Glamorous Stars, I dedicate this one to all of you!

Smiles,

Solara Gordon

CHAPTER ONE

Cassandra Sullivan shook her head and dropped the bedroom window curtain. Cauldron Falls University's Beta-Xi fraternity had out done themselves this time. There was no mistaking the three-foot phallic snow sculptures, thanks to the lamppost illumination marking the property line between her yard and the college campus. Twice, her elderly neighbor, Mrs. Robinson, called asking what Cassandra intended to do about the blatant sexual works of art.

The phone rang again. Ready to tell Mrs. Robinson to take matters into her own hands, Cassandra grabbed the handset. "Now look, Mrs. Robinson, it's too cold out there to do anything about those damn pricks tonight!"

"Excuse me," a deep, distinctly southern male voice asked.

Cassandra gripped the phone harder, hoping she could keep from blushing. "Sorry, Sheriff Knox. Thought it was my neighbor calling again about some kids playing in her yard."

Dakota Knox stood six-foot-five in his bare feet. With his tight jeans that hugged his ass like they were cut exclusively for him and his Stetson pulled low on his head, the man turned many a head as he patrolled Cauldron Falls. In his cowboy boots and uniform shirt with the sleeves rolled up, hot didn't begin to touch the look. Scalding to volcanic boiling might describe the pressure cooker heat he generated every time he got near her. She'd love to run her fingers through his shoulder-length black hair. His Native American features sent her steam meter up another notch closer to cataclysmic meltdown. And the man could dance. Watching his jean-covered ass swing and sway as he two-stepped around Sadie's dance floor or boogied to an eighties disco song at the last Sadie Hawkins full moon dance—Cassandra fanned herself while eyeing the clock. Why was Dakota calling at ten o'clock at night?

Dakota laughed as he heard Cassandra stumble over his next question. He covered the phone's mouthpiece so she couldn't hear him. Lord, the sweet images and erotic thoughts she brought to mind. He was sure her curves would fit snuggled up against him in complimentary ways. He bet she didn't even know he thought about her in that way. "Ah, darlin', what pricks are you talking about?"

1

Cassandra's cough and stutter made him want to reach through the phone and hug her tight to him. Her pale skin and copper curls caused steam he was sure would set off a smoke detector if he weren't careful. Setting off fire alarms and sprinklers was worth the passion and release he'd give both of them if they just had the chance to. . . Another cold burst of wind rattled his office windows and sent another whimper and groan through the ancient heat ducts of his two-story office. The jail was empty due to renovations. His attached living quarters relied on the same boiler the jail and county courthouse used.

Dakota sat upright in his chair. Cassandra clearing her throat ripped him out of his fantasy of them showering together. He smiled at her reply to his earlier question. "The Beta-Xi boys decided the land between their dorm and my place needed some decorating. Uhm. . .you know. . ."

Dakota knew how mischievous the fraternity could be. Stories and rumors flew around town of the wild parties and streaking events from the fraternity's past. He'd already gotten numerous calls about the possible design and description of their snow-sculpting event. There wasn't much he could do until he saw things firsthand. Still, he couldn't resist teasing Cassandra a bit more. "No, I don't know, honey. Tell me about it."

Cassandra held the phone away from her, looking at it as if it had come to life. The man who she'd love to see naked with an erection meant for her just asked her to tell him about the three enormous snow cocks on display outside her bedroom window. Talk about innuendo. Fanning herself vigorously, she placed the phone back to her ear. "I think it's better if you come see this with your own eyes."

Dakota's short chortle caused her to flush even more. His response caught her off guard. "I probably will. See, I need a place to stay tonight. Got room for me there?"

Cassandra coughed, taking a good hard look in the mirror. Her hair stood up in places from her tossing and turning. Her shorty nightgown exposed one shoulder and part of her ample breasts. Never mind she'd forgone panties thinking a night with her sex toys might help her sleep. That hadn't happened thanks to the commotion the artists and her nosey neighbor created.

"Got-got room for you?" There, she said it. Asked the question bugging her from the moment he'd asked it.

"Yes, that extra room you rent out from time to time. Jail's damn boiler finally quit. I need a place to stay until it's fixed. So you got room for me?" Dakota's tone deepened as he spoke. Cassandra gulped, wondering how her prayers got priority on being answered and in the way she fantasized about more than she would ever verbally admit to.

She gulped again, licked her lips and replied. "You're in luck. The room is yours."

Her psyche crowed and flashed several images before her. Dakota naked. . . laying in her bed. His eyes upon her and an open condom packet lay next to him. Her nipples grew taut as she let her mind run with the fantasy forming. One of her hands reached lower toward the apex of her thighs.

Dakota's voice came through the phone low and clear. I'll be there shortly, sweetness. Maybe we'll check out those pricks together one at a time."

Cassandra jumped as silence hummed loudly in her ear. Dakota's last statement had her fanning herself even more. Something about sharing heat to keep warm and ward off the chill set her inner thermostat to boiling.

She paused to pet Dulce-her four-year-old pug-as she put on her slippers and robe. Poor Dulce, the snow was already up to her belly. Getting her to move off the carport when she was outside taking care of nature's call wasn't easy. Shoveling a clear space for her in the yard wouldn't be easy if the drifts continued to increase.

Cassandra glanced toward the window again. Snow blew past, indicating no letup in the storm covering the state. At this rate, the additional ten to twelve inches predicted would come plus several more. Great snowed in and...her mind raced to what she needed to do next. A quick inventory of food, entertainment, and linens topped the list.

Two steps toward her bedroom door, Cassandra stopped. Looking down, she gulped. Her bare legs greeted her. As her gaze moved upward, she nibbled her lip. The short robe covered very little as did her nightgown. Greeting Dakota in her current state of coverage would convey one message. Not one she was sure she wanted to let out yet. Back toward her dresser she moved, untying her robe as she did. She pulled open the top drawer of the dresser closest to the back wall. After rummaging through her other pajamas, she smiled. At the bottom of the drawer, she found what she looked for. The calf-length gown that covered her better. Tossing the robe on the bed, her short nightie quickly followed. She pulled the longer gown on and slipped back into her robe. At least now, she felt like her evening's antics weren't obvious.

Halfway down the hall, her cell phone rang. She reached into her robe's pocket. Empty. Racing back to her bedroom, she grabbed the phone off her dresser on the fourth ring. "Hello," she answered, panting a bit.

"What did I interrupt?" Dakota's voice came through as if he was tight to her and his breath scalded her neck as he pressed against her from the rear.

Fighting the urge to roll her eyes, Cassandra blinked hoping the images flashing through her mind would cease as fast as they arrived. "Nothing more than me checking on things. Making sure your room is ready. Also thought you might want some food."

"Ah, darlin', something *hot* will *do* me great." Dakota's emphasis on hot and do ignited heat that would melt a few snowdrifts she bet. Of course, her internal heat needed to stay right where it was, inside her and under control, as if that was going to happen.

"Why the second call?" she asked, sitting down on the bed, toying with her robe's belt.

"I'm waiting on Mary and Bob from the diner to drop off leftovers for a couple of your neighbors. Storm slowed business down. Need me to bring anything?"

"Not sure. I was going to check after I made up your room. If you have things there, bring them." Cassandra rose. "How soon will you be here?"

"Depends on when Bob and Mary arrive. Probably fifteen minutes after that. Roads are slick. I'm sure many aren't out." Dakota's frustration came through despite his flat laugh.

Cassandra walked to the window and pulled back the curtain. Wind whistled around the window, rattling the half screens and pushing more snow into the fine mesh. "No one appears out on campus from what I can see."

"Good. Nobody is defacing evidence. We've got a cock inspection to conduct when I arrive." Dakota's laughter wrapped around her like a warm blanket that didn't want to let go.

He continued speaking a few moments later. "Anyone in their right mind isn't going to be out. With campus security and the Deputy Police Chief's men patrolling, I think I can take a few hours to sleep and eat."

"Is Deputy Chief Jones back?" Cassandra started pacing. Mentally, Logan Jones's lean five-foot-nine stature snuggled up to her free ear side. His short-cropped brown hair set him apart from Dakota's laid-back look. Logan's hazel eyes glowed when he smiled as though genuine warmth filled him. He looked at a person as he spoke. His attention let a person know they mattered. At the last Sadie Hawkins dance, he'd left more than one woman glowing and happy. The man loved to dance as much as Dakota did. Said it equaled a workout that he couldn't get in due to job duties. That night he hinted at his interest in her as he held her close on their second trip around the dance floor.

"Got in day before yesterday. Picked him up at the airport." Dakota's voice trailed off. Moments of silence began. Cassandra slipped the phone away from her ear ready to end the call when Dakota spoke louder this time. "Sorry. Bob rushed in. Called out and left. Roads slicked up more. I'll be there as soon as safe permits."

Cassandra didn't bother with replying. Dakota's tense statement told her he concentrated on what he needed to do next. Time wasn't measurable at this point. The storm demanded attention without interruption. Getting things ready mattered. She had work to do.

Out in the hall, she stopped in front of the linen closet. She took out a blanket, a set of towels, and a washcloth. Generic toiletry items sat on the second shelf. Good, Dakota could help himself as needed. She moved into the hall bath, clicking on the light as she did. A new toothbrush and tube of toothpaste lay on the counter. An unwrapped bar of soap sat next to them. She laid the towels and washcloth on the counter. The guest room Dakota would occupy sat next to the hall bath.

As she stepped into the room, the furnace kicked on. Heat flowed out the overhead vent. Good, the room's temperature matched her room and the rest of the house. As she lay the blanket on the bed, she glanced around the medium-sized room. No signs of dust or dirt showed. The room and bath were ready. She checked the combination den and office across the hall from the bath. Heat greeted her as she checked the vent. The twin bed was still made up with clean sheets and blankets. Her cousin had canceled his plans to visit last week. Down to the kitchen next.

Another blast of wind rattled the front screen door as Cassandra stepped off the last step of the staircase. Loud humming, obnoxiously high pitched, echoed through the large open-spaced living and dining room combined first floor. She picked up her pace as one more blast of icy air flung itself at the front of the house. The rolled rug along the bottom of the old solid oak door kept the chilled culprit outside.

Midway through the living room, she took inventory of videos and DVDs on hand. Books filled the two bookcases sitting alongside the combination entertainment system. The last two days' newspapers sat on the coffee table as did recent copies of several news magazines. She could see a library donation trip coming soon. Adding to the college library resources as well as giving back to the community, made her job as university head librarian even more enjoyable.

A stack of wood sat next to the fireplace center of the sidewall. Her neighbor's three-story house blocked much of the wind from reaching that side. His privacy fence kept a lot of snow from reaching either of their backyards. Bless Granddad for including the wood-burning stove and oven with the fireplace as part of his graduation gift to her. His and grandma's last postcard indicated they were off to Europe again.

As Cassandra stepped into the kitchen, she looked out the window over the dual sinks. Larger flakes came down rapidly, settling on the outside sill. Great, the storm increased like the forecaster said. Dakota might be here longer than he anticipated. Snowed in together might not....Cassandra pinched her arm, dragging her lust-swollen libido off images of Dakota reclined in her bed. Goodness, she needed to rein in her hormones. At least until she was back in her room where behind a closed door, she could wear out a few more batteries after a round or two with her new vibrator.

What else did she need to check on? Food. She needed to see what she had on hand. She reached for the cabinets closest to the sink. First cabinet yielded baking ingredients. The next one contained oatmeal, dried fruit and containers of nuts. Also a mixture of soups and crackers filled another shelf. She moved next to the refrigerator. Inside it was a large container of homemade chicken stew she prepared for the canceled community Sadie Hawkins social dinner. Biscuits from scratch sat next to the chicken. Two dozen eggs and a gallon of milk occupied the top shelf along with a quart of half-and-half. Food wasn't a problem. She knew the freezer out on the enclosed sun porch held an assortment of meat and seafood. If Dakota wanted coffee, there was a problem.

She had plenty of tea. Pulling her cell phone from her robe pocket, she called Dakota.

"Hey, what's up?" His voice sounded muffled.

"If you haven't left yet, bring coffee."

"No problem. I'm about to leave." Dakota said something that came through garbled as he spoke more.

"Dakota, I didn't hear you." Cassandra upped the volume on her phone.

"Looks like you got two guests. Logan's stuck in town." The rest of Dakota's statement came through distorted with bouts of static and a momentary echo. Then nothing. Cassandra tried redialing him. No ring. Checking how many bars she had didn't help since her network showed none. Great. Best check the landline. She walked across the kitchen to the wall closest to the entry to the front room. She could hear the loud hum of the dial tone as she lifted the receiver. All she could do was sit and wait.

CHAPTER TWO

"I'm not going to ask how you did it." Dakota smiled as he started his pickup truck. Logan sat next to him, stowing one crutch on the rear seat of the pickup truck's king cab and the other next to him. "I'm glad you're okay."

"Icy steps and a little shit named Chuy." Logan leaned forward, rubbing his knee and calf. "Mrs. Abernathy's Chihuahua got loose again."

"You went to help." Dakota looked at him, not bothering to suppress his wide grin. Dakota's shrug didn't help.

"How could I not? Mrs. Abernathy came running up crying." Logan slumped down in the heated leather seat. "Damn crazy mutt's got this pussy thing going on. He's gotta chase the neighbor's cat."

"Yeah I know. We promised to serve and protect. Gods, some days are worse than others." Dakota eased the truck out of the emergency room's parking lot and onto the street as he continued. "Did you catch Chuy?"

"Little shit ran up to me and licked my face as I lay on the steps. Damn mutt tried to piss on me." Logan heaved an exasperated sigh.

"Thankfully, Mrs. Abernathy's EMT-trained nephew checked on her. Or you might still be on those steps cussing Chuy out."

"Love the new electronic x-ray equipment. A tech in Coeur 'd'Alene read it while I lay on the table." Logan noted Dakota gripped the steering wheel tighter. "You okay?"

"Road's slicker than I expected. We're almost to Cassandra's." Dakota skidded to a stop midway through the intersection of Main Street and River Crossing Highway.

"Damn, this storm is racking the shit out of things. The river bridge is probably one sheet of ice." Logan pulled himself upright in his seat. "Cassandra's?"

"Yes," Dakota ground out. He looked in the rearview mirror. He kept looking as if something intently had his attention.

Logan tried to turn, but his seatbelt and the crutch next to him had him at a disadvantage. Rolling down his window, he looked in the side mirror. "Looks like there's a patch of ice or snow under the wheels."

"Fuck!" Dakota cussed, rolling down his window. Snow, accompanied by another burst of wind, blew in, chilling the cab's interior. "I'm gonna back up and try easing around the buildup."

"I'd offer to push, but. . ." Logan touched his crutch.

"Hang on. If this doesn't do it, I've got another idea." Dakota put the truck into reverse, slowly easing the truck backward. Logan kept watching in the side mirror. The patch he noticed disappeared from view.

Snow and ice flew as Dakota tried to move forward. The back end of the truck fishtailed, sliding left and right several times before Dakota cussed again. "Double shit! This is gonna take two steps."

"What ya got in mind?" Logan asked, unfastening his seat belt.

"Hold on. This needs sure footing." Dakota held up his hand. "I'm glad this truck isn't manual."

"What now?" Logan rolled up his window.

"There's a cover for the middle console that converts the front into a bench seat." Dakota turned around, peering into the rear seat section. "I think I see it."

Logan pulled his keys out of his pocket. "Hang on. I got a light." He clicked on the key chain flashlight he carried. "I see it. Bring your hand down to the left."

"Thanks, I got it." Dakota snapped the cover in place. "I'm gonna push and you drive." Dakota turned, opening his door. "Sorry for the pain. Had to be your ankle Chuy messed up."

"Pain is worth it. Let's do it." Logan began sliding across the center portion of the seat onto the console cover.

Dakota rolled down his window before opening the door more. "Hold off until you see my hand go up. Ease on the gas after you're in drive. Glad I changed into my hikers."

"Got ya. Stop once we're clear." Logan got behind the wheel, fastening the seatbelt as Dakota closed the door.

Ten minutes passed as the back-and-forth battle with the snow and ice threatened to win. Dakota came back to the front of the truck. "We're almost clear. It's real icy. We gotta make it this time."

Logan held up two thumbs, smiling. Dakota's spattered parka spoke of things on his end. Dakota nodded and made his way back along the truck bed. Logan waited until he saw Dakota's hand. Foot off brake, on the gas . . .the truck shot forward two feet before he could stop without skidding more. He glanced in the rearview mirror. Dakota gingerly got up from where he laid in the middle of the intersection amidst the ice and snow they moved off of. The huge scowl on his face said what he felt. As he approached the truck, he started laughing. Logan swallowed as he put the truck in park. Had Dakota lost it?

"Oh man dude! I musta looked like one silly fool. Flaying my arms and trying to stay standing." Dakota wiped his face with the bandana he pulled out of his pocket. "Reminds me of learning to ice skate."

Logan slid back into the passenger seat, chuckling as he fastened his seat belt. "Oh shit, yes! The time we went out for hockey."

"Spent more time on our asses than standing up." Dakota jumped in the cab, fastened his seat belt and put the truck into gear.

"You all right?" Logan asked.

"Yeah. Nothing a hot shower and sleep won't cure." Dakota hunched his shoulders as he drove. "Or one of Cassandra's massages."

"Massage? Cassandra?" Logan turned as best he could toward Dakota.

"Oh yeah. She went for her license in massage therapy a couple months back." Dakota flashed a grin and kept on driving.

"Is she quitting her librarian job?" Logan gripped the door handle hard. He winced at the harshness of his tone. Still, he didn't like Dakota knowing more about Cassandra than he did.

"Nah. One of the free classes the college offered. She went with her best friend Maggie Nickerson." Dakota glanced at him.

Logan wondered if he frowned based on Dakota's next statements.

"Take it easy dude. I heard about it from Mary. Bob went along as her patient for the test." Dakota glanced back at him as he slowed again.

"She's an independent woman. I talked to her about my interest last Sadie Hawkins."

"You know I'm interested too. I don't think she knows we both want her." Dakota pulled into the combination convenience store and gas station close to the edge of campus. "Hang tight. I'll be back in a few."

"What you need?" Logan asked, slouching in his seat. His ankle started throbbing.

"Coffee and condoms." Dakota slid out of the cab, slamming his door shut before Logan could respond.

Logan rolled down his window and leaned out. "Coffee and what?" he called out.

Dakota trotted back to the passenger side of the truck. "Condoms bro'. Gotta protect *our* lady. Being prepared never hurts."

Logan groaned as Dakota's smile widened. "You think she's going to go for us both?"

"We won't know until we ask. Now will we?" Dakota held up one finger as Logan opened his mouth. "Prepared. No means no if she refuses."

"Okay. We'll talk about this later." Logan closed his window, watching Dakota trot into the store. Drumming his fingers on the door, Logan wondered what had happened during his two-month army reserve assignment out of town. How close had Dakota and Cassandra gotten? Had they dated like Dakota indicated in a few of their conversations? Military reserves field training out in the woods without phone or computer access limited communications. It also forced him to focus on what he wanted. What were his desires and needs? Damn storm and Chuy hadn't given Dakota and him time to talk. Their initial conversations on sharing Cassandra happened close to him leaving for training.

Inside the store, Dakota walked to the back where he knew Logan couldn't see him. Maybe cell phone reception would be better since the corner of the store faced one of the mobile phone providers' towers along the peaks separating Cauldron Falls from the Montana Idaho border. He pulled his phone out of his parka pocket. Two bars out of four. He might be able to get a call into Cassandra before he and Logan arrived.

One ring. Two rings. "Come on sweetness, please answer," he muttered, acting like he was filling out a lottery ticket form as he phoned. On the third ring, she answered.

"Dakota?" Her voice sounded sleepy like he'd awakened her.

"Yes. Logan and I are almost there. I'm at the convenience store. You need anything else besides coffee?"

Her muffled yawn brought a smile to him. *Oh yes get your rest now. Later you're gonna need it.* Damn he needed to get his mind off sex. Not that it was a bad thing. Permission was essential.

"Nothing else. Unless you're one of those flavored coffee people." Cassandra's next yawn convinced him that tonight was about sleep and not the discussion he and Logan had in mind.

"Okay. By the way, Logan is on crutches. Mrs. Abernathy's Chihuahua. . ." Cassandra cut him off.

"Chuy's reputation runs rampant. Come in through the kitchen door. There's no snow on the steps."

"All right, see you in a few." Dakota rung off as he made his way through the aisles picking up what he needed—a large can of coffee, a box of condoms and a pack of colored balloons.

The clerk smiled at him as he rang him up. Dakota managed to keep his poker face present. Let the man have his thoughts. Might be all he had if the storm continued. He might be working twelve hours before his relief showed up. Dakota nodded as the clerk handed him his change.

"Have a good evening Sheriff," the clerk stated before he reached for the next customer's merchandise.

"Yeah, thanks." Dakota moved forward fighting back the grin threatening to curl his lips. Sometimes letting folks' imaginations run where they liked was fun. Hell, if he'd done half of what some of the rumors said he had, his reputation would. . tarnished didn't begin to touch how tinged and very smudged he'd be. As he reached the truck, he caught a good look at Logan slumped in the seat with a scowl longer than a moping toddler wore when his mama put 'em on a time-out. Frowns could be turned right side up and into smiles. This was a 'I'm feeling super sorry for myself' glower that even three hands of strip poker with everyone starting out stark naked wouldn't dent. Shit, maybe his joke wasn't going to work. Dakota wasn't giving up.

"Here, hold this," Dakota said, opening the door and tossing the bag at Logan.

Logan reached for the bag fumbling as he tried to sit up and grab the bag simultaneously. The bag hit his arm. Then his chest before the contents spilled out onto his lap. The can of coffee rolled off his lap and landed on the floor between his feet. He took a hold of the other items. He glanced at the condom package. Looked at Dakota, opened his mouth to speak, shook his head, and closed his mouth. The second item he drew up, leaned forward, holding it almost against the windshield.

"What are these for?" Logan knew the moment he asked, he shouldn't have.

"Well, you know extras never hurt." Dakota pulled out of the parking lot, easing onto the street.

"Extra what?" Logan knew he trudged into something deeper as Dakota looked at him.

"Condoms?" Dakota quipped. He kept looking straight ahead.

Logan closed his eyes, wondering if he dared go further. Dakota's sense of humor ran in ironical flows. The quirky grin he wore as he glanced away from his driving said something was up.

"These aren't going to fit. They're too damn small." Logan tossed the package of balloons in the bag. He stuffed the bag on the seat between them.

"Got ya," Dakota retorted. "You stopped feeling sorry for yourself for a few."

"Thanks. I needed that." Logan sat up more in his seat. "When you're in charge, relying on someone else ain't easy."

"Our jobs are equals. We work well together and know how to use that." Dakota slowed as he came to blinking stoplights. "Great, the storm takes another hit."

"Damn, this is hitting harder than they predicted." Logan started to roll down his window.

"Don't bother. We're almost there." Dakota leaned forward, wiping condensation off the windshield. He started laughing the more he wiped. "Damn they did it good."

"What?" Logan leaned forward, looking to where Dakota pointed. "Beta-Xi. Gotta love their originality."

"No wonder Cassandra is irritated. Those can't be missed. Talk about stand out." Dakota turned onto the narrow side street running between where the campus started and the residential area next to it.

Logan snorted. "With the wind chill and subzero temps, those suckers are gonna be hard."

Dakota started coughing as he slowly drove down the street. "A bit of pun and innuendo there."

"It's the truth." Logan chortled. "I think the name on that mailbox says C. Sullivan."

"I see it. I'm going to park in Cassandra's carport." Dakota pulled forward onto the driveway's apron. "Hold on while I square up with the driveway. "

Dakota backed up until he could safely turn into the drive and park behind Cassandra's car. "Without the snow emergency, getting in here might be harder."

"Yeah, kids parking everywhere they can. County ordinance will see to that." Logan started to unfasten his seatbelt.

"Good. Fire department complained again about issues with illegal parking in front of the hydrants." Dakota reached out, touched Logan's arm, and spoke more. "Can you slide over this way to get out?"

"Did it once, I can do it again. I ain't driving with this foot. Damn it's throbbing." Logan took ahold of his crutches. "Those steps look easy."

Dakota nodded as he opened his door. "Yes. The crutches will do okay if you take it easy and slow."

"Yeah, just what I need more pain." Logan eased onto the running board, ready to step out.

"Lean on me bro'. And take it slow. We'll get you inside as safely as we can." Dakota leaned on the side of the truck ready to steady Logan as he placed his good foot on the concrete. Crutches under his arms, Logan inched his way forward. Wobbling, he stood, reaching for the door. Dakota slipped his arm around his waist, tugging him to him.

"Ready?" Dakota asked, taking a small step forward.

"Let's go for it." Logan took a hop and shuffled forward leaning on his crutches as Dakota stepped. Ten minutes later, they reached the stairs as Cassandra opened the door.

"Welcome. Come on in." Cassandra moved away from the door, giving Dakota enough room to ease Logan inside.

CHAPTER THREE

"Here you go, Logan." Cassandra pushed the lightweight wheelchair her granddad had used when he broke his ankle toward him.

"Do I look like I need that?" Logan caught the inside of his bottom lip between his teeth hoping to prevent the hiss of pain barreling up his throat from escaping. His ankle throbbed worse than a jackhammer on a hot summer day thumping pavement without earplugs in. His head hurt from lack of sleep and food.

"Don't matter if you do or don't." Dakota tossed in his concern. "You've used your foot more than the doctor said to. Keep it up and cast time happens."

Logan inhaled, swallowing his retort. Last thing he needed was six weeks in a cast because he messed up the swollen ligaments due to a lousy sprain. His luck, Mrs. Abernathy would bring Chuy to visit saying both of 'em needed cheering up. Piss ant Chihuahua. Just what he didn't need, a yappy thinking he's a cuddly lap dog trying to wash his face again.

Sighing, Logan hobbled toward where Cassandra stood. "Keep it steady. I'm ready to crash."

"Grab the table and wait. I'll come to you." Cassandra started pushing the chair toward him. What he really wanted to do was sprawl on the table and snore. The pain pills the clinic gave him were kicking in full strength. His ability to stay awake wasn't going to last too long. Rocking back and forth on his good leg only stressed it more, adding to the tight muscles screaming with each move. Keeping his balance wasn't easy. He must look like a drunk trying to show his sobriety. Wasn't happening.

Dakota came up beside him. "Take it easy for a moment, okay? Sit down if you need to."

Logan looked down as chair legs came into view. "Thanks. I think I need that." He dropped into the regular chair Dakota steadied close to him.

Cassandra stopped as he looked up. Her ruffled hair made him think of a hen with her comb up as she watched over her chicks. God, the drugs must be kicking in more. He was ready to giggle at his own dumb thoughts and images.

Logan looked up again. Cassandra's gaze met his. Was that mirth that he caught flashing over her? Had her eyes glowed and a swift grin curled her lips before he blinked? Logan looked down lest the room started spinning again.

Dakota cleared his throat. "I've got a couple things to bring in. You can handle?" He pointed to Logan. The front desk clerk at the clinic mentioned the pain meds were strong along with causing drowsiness. The doctor on duty stated light food for the first eight hours then regular as Logan could tolerate. Poor guy wasn't going to be happy thumping around in the boot they sent with him. Couldn't blame him.

"Yes, he's fine. I'll get him started on the stew I heated." Cassandra made her way around the table, crouching so she came into Logan's line of vision.

"I want you to stay put." She held up her hand. "You've got to eat."

"Not sure I-I c-can." Logan's hand shook as he brought it up. "Make the room stop spinning."

Cassandra stood up. She cupped her hand around Logan's chin and tipped his head back until he looked at her. "One way is to eat. Bread and some stew will help."

"Cup please." Logan mumbled. "Butter and bread?"

"You got it. No more looking down. Sooner you eat, the better you'll feel." Cassandra made her way to the stove, glancing back over her shoulder twice. Each time Logan waved to her as best he could. His hand didn't shake as bad on the second wave. At least his color returned instead of looking pasty and flushed.

"Half a mug of stew coming up. Chicken vegetable will go down easy. Sip 'cuz it's hot." Cassandra filled the second mug two-thirds full. Dakota would eat like he wasn't sure when he would again. Twelve-hour shifts didn't allow for much. Eat, sleep and patrol. Had he heard on his request to Coeur d'Alene for additional funding?

Logan picked up the spoon Cassandra set on the table next to the mug. His hand trembled as he stirred the stew. She wanted to help. Offering assistance probably wasn't a good idea. All she could think of was spoon-feeding him. Not a good idea. Logan didn't give a damn about machismo masculinity. He described himself as a New Age male. One who didn't mind help when he asked for it or the offer of the same. Someone assuming they knew what he needed. .

.well, she'd seen his reaction when two of his staff decided to straighten up his office while he attended a conference. Not a good turn of events.

As she started back toward the table with the buttered bread, a loud thud sounded. The door rattled. She laid the bread on the table close to Logan and trotted to the door. Dakota stood on the steps trying to balance an overflowing basket against the door while he reached for the doorknob. In his other hand, he clutched two bags. Cassandra shook her head. Dakota and laundry, his never-ending problem. He never seemed to get it all caught up. Goddess, single men.

She pulled the door open, standing behind it, as a brisk breeze whistled up the carport scattering snow on the steps. Dakota set the basket on the floor laying the bags on top of it.

"Thanks. One more item. Coffee can!" He turned ready to move down the stairs.

"Okay I'm going to push the door to. Please latch it when you come in." Cassandra didn't wait for Dakota's reply. Logan needed help more than Dakota did.

Back at the table, Logan sat holding the mug with both hands. He raised it, slurped twice, and set the mug down. He glanced at her. Sleep claimed him more. His lopsided grin reminded her of the first time she met him. Lunchtime at the diner after a dental appointment. Novocain hadn't worn off. All he could do was wave and grin.

"How you doing?" She asked, reaching for the mug.

"Almost done." He picked up the slice of homemade bread. He took a bite. His eyes closed as he chewed. Three more bites, and he reopened his eyes. "Good. More please."

Cassandra nibbled her lips, trying to keep a straight face. Logan's request reminded her of her three-year-old nephew asking for seconds. She glanced in the mug as she picked it up. Most of the vegetables remained in the bottom along with a good-sized hunk of chicken. Maybe she could get the chicken down him if she put it on the next slice of bread. "I'll get you another slice. How about I cut up the chicken and make you a half sandwich?"

"Okay," Logan managed to get out in between yawns. "Need a bit more to eat."

Cassandra smiled. Logan could put the food away if it was something he liked. Dakota too. The way both ate, she understood why they jogged three times a week, weather permitting. Their fave jogging route took them down past the historical mill on Old Creek Road. Many of Cauldron Falls' single women drove down the road at a pace that mimicked a snail's if he had a turbine engine as his power source trailing them.

The first time Logan and Dakota caught her watching them jog, Maggie drove. Neither of them stalked men like some of the females around town felt the need to do. However, a dare sometimes needed an answer. Why Maggie chose the one to lead the pack driving slowly down Old Creek Road admiring the gaggle of male joggers she didn't know. Something about it felt right continued to be Maggie's answer. Several of the males stopped as they got to where the road dead-ended and the cars full of females parked. Dakota and Logan made their way up to her and Maggie followed by Josh and Adam. Josh and Adam spoke with Maggie while Dakota and Logan talked with her. All four men topped the list of prime catches as husbands. Rumors abounded that two men to every woman in town made sharing a necessity. Then there was pack law. Living amongst shape shifters could liven things up. This far north, the rules and regulations governing separation between species blurred. They were one of the counties that didn't issue hunting licenses. No shooting your neighbor unknowingly.

"Okay, I'll get you going in a moment. How about some tea to warm you up?" Cassandra reached into the cabinet where she kept several boxes of herbal teas. Chamomile would settle Logan's stomach while also soothing him into the sleep his pain meds appeared to be doing.

"No caffeine. Doc said need sleep and rest. Sandwich?" Logan's voice sounded like he was halfway to nodding off where he sat.

"Coming right now." Cassandra quickly shredded the chicken onto the buttered bread, cut it in half, and placed it on a plate. She dumped the remaining vegetables back in the pan holding the other half of the container of stew she'd warmed. As she turned, the door flew open. Dakota rushed inside shoving the door shut with his foot.

"Damn that wind is vicious. Practically a whiteout. Checked on the elderly couple across the street." Dakota took his Stetson off his head, shaking it before placing it on a peg of the coat on the wall next to the door. "Also next door.

Both are good. Brought wood up to their doors for them and the food Bob and Mary left with me for them."

He started unzipping his parka. He looked up to where Cassandra stood watching him. He smiled as he shrugged out of his parka. "I'm fine. Took a spill getting the truck over a patch of ice on Main Street. It needs washing like I do."

"Looks like most of your clothes need it too. Have you got any clean items you can wear?" Cassandra set Logan's sandwich down next to him. Logan picked it up and took a bite.

"Glad to see you eating, dude. I tossed your stuff from your locker in with mine." Dakota hung his parka on the coat pegs near the door. "At least you got your jacket off."

"Yes, now as to clean items. What do you have that either of you can wear?" Cassandra started toward the basket, shaking her head.

"Hey, don't tsk me," Dakota teased. "Boiler out, no hot water to wash anything."

"There's cold water, you know." Cassandra picked up the basket, looking at the two bags lying on top of it.

Dakota trotted over, taking both in hand. "Personal."

Cassandra's arched eyebrow and chagrin came through. He knew she partially believed him. "I'll leave it be. Now what do you need out of here?"

Dakota laid the bags on the table and reached for the basket. "Couple of t-shirts, briefs, and jogging shorts. Probably sweats once they're clean."

"Socks," Logan ground out. "Hate cold feet."

Dakota smiled as Cassandra faced him. "For sure."

"Get out what you need. I'll start the washer in the morning."

Dakota nodded, placing the basket on the table. He dug down and pulled out what he needed. Glancing at Logan, he spoke. "I'll get your boot out of the truck tomorrow. Hope you don't mind sharing clothes."

Logan yawned and spoke. "Clean and wearable is good."

"How you feeling, Logan?" Dakota asked, handing Cassandra the basket.

"Sleepy. Want tea. Then bed." Logan pointed to the crutches close to the door. "Gonna need help with those."

Cassandra took the basket from Dakota. "Think you can make it up the steps?"

Logan's mumbled yes followed Dakota's reply. "I'll make sure he gets upstairs."

"Got ya. One of you is in the den on the twin bed." Cassandra stepped into the laundry out of earshot as Dakota sat down next to Logan.

"Take the room closest to the bath. Easier to get to it if you need it." Dakota leaned in and spoke lower. "Don't worry about things tonight. Just rest and sleep."

Logan nodded. "Forget tea. Too tired."

Dakota rose, got the crutches, and had Logan standing by the time Cassandra came back into the kitchen. "I'll get him upstairs. Be back down for food in a few."

"Here, you need these." Cassandra held out two pairs of slippers. "Don't need either of you slipping."

"Thanks." Dakota grabbed the bags off the table, stuffing one pair of slippers in them. The other he laid on the table. He turned toward the clothes he needed.

Cassandra held out a plastic grocery bag. "Makes things easier."

Dakota murmured his thanks and leaned Logan against him. Getting to bed would take a while longer. Sleep might give him a merry chase before they embraced each other. Didn't matter. Safe, warm, and snowbound with his best friend, and the woman they decided to share wasn't looking so bad.

CHAPTER FOUR

Rousing some, Cassandra shielded her eyes. Had Dakota forgotten to turn off the hall light? He'd pulled her door to after he walked her upstairs post consuming two bowls of stew and four slices of homemade bread and butter. He mentioned needing to write reports and wanting to read before turning in. She'd seen the pages of instructions the medic provided for Logan's care. Dakota said he wanted to go over them a couple of times before he lay down. Logan ended up in the guest room across the hall from Dakota.

Blinking, her vision cleared. Light filtered in through the partially open blinds. The sky looked much the same as it had yesterday. She couldn't tell if more snow fell. Not that she cared. Snuggling back under the blankets with sleep as her companion sounded superb. Rolling over, she glanced toward the clock sitting atop her nightstand. 10:15 A.M.! Lord, she never slept this late. Grabbing the covers, she tossed them back ready to sit up and. . . and do what? The storm left over two feet of snow last report she and Dakota listened to around midnight. Even then, the forecaster said another storm was backing up near the Canadian border, threatening to stall the current one over the area. The university closed. Relief personnel were on duty to feed and watch over the students in the four on-campus dorms. The only work that awaited her was laundry, cooking breakfast, and keeping Dakota and Logan company. Snuggling back into the blankets, taking a bit of time for her was a luxury she could afford at the moment. Cuddling Dulce close to her as she invited sleep to reclaim her wasn't a bad addition. Dulce deserved some pats and scratches. She'd kept out of the way last night. She adored Dakota as well as Logan. Her curly tail didn't wag much but she wiggled when someone she liked was in the house.

Taking one deep breath after another, Cassandra visualized each muscle relaxing. Slowly she relaxed back into a dreamlike state. Somewhere between deep sleep and the start of Rem, her breathing evened as she sunk lower into the dream visuals claiming her.

Dakota stood in the doorway. His shirt hung open, exposing part of his chest. The patch of hair she could make out peeked out from the edges of where his shirt plackets lay close together. His jeans rode low on his hips creating the

21

illusion he hadn't bothered zipping them closed. Perhaps the button that held them closed otherwise wasn't secured. Next to him, Logan lounged against the door jam. He slung his shirt over his shoulder, leaving his chest bare. Shirtless, his chest hair matched that close to the top of his waistband, teasing her to check out the inverted v that trailed down into his. . .

Sounds of metal banging, followed by a loud thud that shook the floor, rocked Cassandra from her dreamy dozing.

"Shit!" blasted her out of her sleepy state. Logan's voice echoed down the hall. She scrambled out from under the sheet and blanket and rushed into the hall. She squinted as the bright light of the hall greeted her. There was no mistaking the scene in front of her.

Logan stood in the bathroom doorway clutching the door with both hands. His crutches and the bathroom throw rug adorned the hall floor. As she glanced toward the end of the hall, Dakota stepped into the hall shielding his eyes. Cassandra blinked, hoping her mouth didn't hang open because she wasn't sure her mind hadn't slipped back into sleep again. Both men were naked. Buck ass naked. She swallowed. Willed herself to take a deep breath. Neither Dakota nor Logan seemed phased by their undressed state.

Dakota moved into the hall as naturally as if nudity between them was commonplace. "What happened?" He bent down, reaching for the crutches. If he bent over more, she'd get a bird's eye view of his ass and another of his cock and balls. The first look proved her imagination didn't do him justice.

Then there was Logan. Tight abs and a cock that rivaled her fantasies. His pubic hair matched the hair on his head. His pecs reminded her of Olympic weightlifters. Oh goodness, what her psyche would do with this added info.

"Crutches got caught up in the rug." Logan looked up smiling. "Sorry for the noise, Cassandra."

Dakota untangled the rug from the crutches. "Easy does it. Did you hit your ankle?"

"No, caught the door in time." Logan started to reach for the crutch Dakota held.

"Hold on. Let me come to you." Dakota stood up and stepped toward Logan.

Cassandra licked her lips hoping to resist the urge to comb her hands through her hair or fan herself. The two men she fantasized about repeatedly stood before her nude, gloriously nude. No need for guessing what they might look like. Her fantasy stood a few feet from her. Side by side, two of the most sought-after males in town stood nude and didn't appear to care. Her gaze raked over them as if committing to memory every nuance to ensure her dreams and fantasies didn't lack added fuel.

Logan cleared his throat breaking her concentration. She lingered on their faces this time as her view cleared again. Dakota smiled this time as well. They caught her purusing them. Cassandra gulped the retort waiting to blurt out. They were nude and nonchalant about it. She could be too. Couldn't she?

"Things are under control here. I'll be downstairs in a few. Come down for breakfast." She turned around, walked back into her room, and shut the door. As she crossed the room, she caught her reflection in the full-length mirror hanging on the wall closest to the master bathroom. Flushed from her cheeks down to the v-neckline of her nightgown, there was no mistaking how turned-on she was. Had Dakota and Logan noticed?

Adding to things, Dulce sat midway between everything wearing a doggy smile with her pink tongue hanging out. "Dulce, come," Cassandra called as she cracked open her door. Dulce barely got through the door before Cassandra clicked it shut.

Dakota shook his head and handed Logan his other crutch. "Let me know when you're steady."

Logan winced as he put the other crutch under his arm. "I'll be glad when the swelling is down enough for me to wear the boot. Hopping on one foot isn't easy."

Dakota chuckled. "I hear ya. Take it easy coming into the hall." He kicked the throw rug out of Logan's path.

Moving ahead of him, Dakota made his way to the room where he left Logan sleeping last night after a quick late-night sponge bath. The towels they used to soak up the water on the floor hung over the edge of the tub and shower curtain rod. Dakota's towel hung on the towel rack with his washcloth. Next to it hung the still-damp bath mat. A shower and sponge bath took more water than either of them anticipated.

"I fell asleep waiting for you to finish showering." Logan spoke as he inched his way across the hall toward the room he occupied.

"I laid on the bed hoping to get another burst of energy." Dakota stepped inside Logan's room. "No such luck."

"Yup, we fell asleep nude." Logan snickered. "Not an issue at home I guess."

"I think Cassandra got an eyeful she hadn't expected." Dakota offered as Logan sat on the bed.

"She was flushed and quiet. I caught her giving me the once over. I think she did you too." Logan caught the clothes Dakota tossed to him.

"Oh, I caught her." Dakota started toward the door eager to pull on clothes and talk with Cassandra.

"Probably time to talk about our mutual courtship plans." Logan offered.

Dakota stopped at the bedroom door. He glanced back at Logan. "Getting her buy-in might be a better idea."

Logan's muffled reply followed. "At least see if she's interested."

Dakota smiled, shaking his head as he exited the room. Cassandra's perusal of them told of her interest. From a sexual standpoint, attraction was a great thing to build on. Chemistry helped to a point. Taking the stakes to a higher level might not work if they moved too fast.

He moved through the hall quickly. He could hear the shower running in the master bath. Images of Cassandra nude, sandwiched between him and Logan as they washed her, flashed into being. Her lush ample curves begged for a caress and touch. Taking the bar of soap from her, he lathered his hands knowing where he wanted to place them first. Sounds distracted his thoughts. Cracks and pops sounded. A loud crunch followed. He moved to the window, pulled back the curtains and peered out.

Icicles resembling bear trap teeth hung from the peak of the roof and gutters. Another pop sounded and two smaller tendrils of ice dashed toward the snow piled below. The wind whistled between the small openings in amongst the icy stalactites. It was like the cold reached through the storm window and the inside pane wanting to envelope him in its chill. Dakota dropped the curtain. He moved to the dresser taking the briefs and shorts off the top. Pulling them on, he wondered if the heat he felt flooding off Cassandra as she gave him the once over would double, maybe triple, and flow over the three of them; embracing them in a cascade of desire that warmed their interiors as well as the house overall. Easing his feet into the slippers Cassandra gave him the night before, he wondered where her thoughts were. Logan and he would find out soon enough.

Cassandra picked up the bar of soap working the lather between her hands. Her nipples ached as much as her clit. Both swelled with a need that pinged through her at a popcorn rate. This wasn't an easy quick orgasm fix. Soaping her fingers to slip them over and around her clit hadn't helped from the moment she reached between her legs to wash. The need rushed back into her like an out-of-control rapid brush fire. Control required her composure return. Fat chance that would happen given every time she closed her eyes visions of Dakota and Logan nude swarmed her. Temporary relief might work. The need to feel a warm male anatomy filling her as an equally delicious hot male pressed against her nipped at her.

Pinching her nipple between her fingers, she rolled it back and forth. Her other hand slid lower slicked with the remaining soap sluicing down her as water poured over her. Two strokes across her throbbing clit. Another edged her tighter to hotter need. Taking her slickest finger, she began rapid short strokes over and around her clit. Closing her eyes, she let her mind wander taking her where her thoughts went.

Dakota kneeled in front of her, pressing his face closer to her mons. His tongue licked between her swollen nether lips seeking out her taut clit. She pressed her hips forward feeling his face heating her thighs as he found her clit. One lap, then another followed by more swelled her tiny nub with need that inched her closer to a climax. Behind her, Logan pressed against her. He nipped her neck as he pressed tighter to her.

"I want to bury my cock deep in you," Logan hotly whispered in her ear. "Feel you pulse and throb as Dakota brings you to orgasm."

Cassandra opened her mouth, pulling in air. Her fingers moved faster over her clit. She squeezed her nipple harder, twisting it quicker. Her fantasy took on a new level of play.

Logan firmly gripped her hips and pushed against her. His directions accented his movements. "Ah, bend just a little. Yes, push back against me. Slowly take me in. Gods you're tight."

Dakota's tongue stroked her faster as Logan began pumping in and out of her. Her hands encircled her breasts, finding her nipples. Plucking and twisting she couldn't move as Logan tightened his hold on her hips, moving faster and fuller into her with each thrust. Dakota cupped her ass cheeks close to where her thighs and ass met. His hold kept her from going anywhere. A thrust, a lick, a pluck, a pull and...

"*Oh my!*" she groaned as one wave, followed by another, tossed her up and down deeper into the pulsating bliss her climax brought. More shudders and pulses raced over her pooling deep within her. Want filled her with a deep unfulfilled desire. As her shudders slowed and lessened, physical hunger ramped up its demand. Her stomach growled. And a headache threatened to end the partial bliss she felt.

Shutting off the shower, Cassandra stepped out onto the bath mat. Toweling dry, she let her mind wander more. Keeping her thoughts sedate wasn't going to happen until she faced Dakota and Logan dressed. Even then, things were going to be different. What direction would this go? Could she answer what she wanted? What her expectations were?

A hard knock on her bedroom door discontinued her thought process.

"Yes, "she answered, cracking the door open slightly.

"Wanted to make sure you were all right," Dakota said.

"Yes, I'll be down in a few minutes."

"Okay, Logan and I are going down now."

She closed her door and leaned against it, listening for the sounds of steps descending the stairs. They came. She let go a sigh that sounded like relief. Could she honestly say the tension the earlier incident ignited was any different? Different from what? Her lust for the two men who awaited her downstairs? Or did she want more? She wasn't sure. Did Logan and Dakota know? What a loaded topic!

She could muse on the topic with only her side for input. That didn't shine any light on how Dakota or Logan felt. They had responses that mattered. No, the solution wouldn't come with the flip of a coin or a quick discussion. For now, clothes and food mattered. Cassandra quickly pulled on jeans and a short-sleeved sweatshirt over her panties and bra. She slipped her bare feet into a pair of sheepskin-lined moccasins.

The morning paper could wait until the snow melted to find it. Hotter and spicier topics lurked around the sidelines, waiting their chance at infamy. Cassandra opened her bedroom door, took a deep breath, and moved into the hall. She could hear Logan and Dakota's muffled voices coming from the kitchen. She couldn't make out what they said. She'd know soon enough what they animatedly discussed.

Dakota helped Logan down the last step of the staircase. "Stand still. I'll get the wheelchair." He started toward the kitchen.

"Do I really need that?" Logan called out as Dakota reached the door.

"After the rug, you gotta ask?" Dakota didn't wait for a reply. He went on into the kitchen. As he pushed the chair into the dining area off the living room, he glanced toward the window. Snow covered parts of the lower panes.

CHAPTER FIVE

Dakota nodded toward the window as he reached Logan. "Storm walloped us last night."

Logan looked at the window as he sat in the chair. "Probably blew a lot. I heard the wind whistling a couple of times."

"I'll check things out later. I need coffee." Dakota wheeled Logan into the kitchen.

"I hate feeling useless. How can I help?" Logan tried looking back at him.

"By sitting still for now. I think I remember where Cassandra keeps the coffee maker." Dakota opened a few cabinets before he found what he sought, a small coffee maker. "Where did the coffee can end up?"

"On the counter." Logan pointed toward the sink and counter area.

"Thanks. You probably want a cup, too." Dakota measured water and coffee into the server. "I don't know how soon Cassandra will be down. We need to talk."

"Yes, I got that from her reaction." Logan leaned on his hands, cupping his chin.

Dakota pulled out a chair and sat down. "I'm not sure dropping the courtship idea on her is good."

"We're here. Pack law says we have to declare our interest." Logan laid one of his hands on the table.

"Yes and mark her as claimed. A night of passion with each of us." Dakota rose and went to the refrigerator. "Has she dated you?"

"A couple of shared lunches. Remember, I wasn't here."

"I know. We had dinner and saw a movie a few times." Dakota set a carton of eggs on the stove. Next to them, he laid a loaf of bread, three potatoes, some chili peppers, and a jar of mango pineapple salsa. "Southwestern omelet?"

"Is there any cheese or sausage to add to it?" Logan sat up.

Dakota chortled. "Food got your attention?"

"Look, you can cook. I'm stuck with takeout or frozen dinners at home. Or simple quick recipes." Logan shoved back from the table, maneuvering the chair around it.

"No wonder you were anxious to get down here." Dakota moved the food items to the counter. "I'll check on the sausage and cheese in a moment. Locate some tea for Cassandra."

"How do you know where things are?" Logan paused as he opened a cabinet beneath the counter.

"Stayed here when I first got into town." Dakota leaned against the counter. "Cassandra's granddad Earl interviewed me for my job."

"Me too. You think we're set up?" Logan held a box of tea in his hand.

"If we were, so what? Good tea choice." Dakota walked over to take the box. He continued speaking. "Mortals and shapeshifters homesteaded the town. Nothing wrong with a bit of matchmaking."

"What? No matchmaking I'm aware of." Logan held out the box of tea.

"Not per se, dude. Earl enjoys poker and chess. I bested him twice during the diner's lunch tournaments." Dakota started filling the electric tea kettle with water.

"Yes, her granddad plays a crafty poker game. He sat in on a tourney down at the community center last fall." Logan pointed to the eggs. "Can I get those cracked for you?"

"Sure." Dakota placed a bowl and the egg carton on the counter. "Six of them please. Toss the shells into the garbage disposal side." He continued where he left off. "Earl introduced me to Cassandra when I interviewed. Got to know her more thanks to the tournaments and running into her in town."

He began rummaging in the refrigerator. "Any kind of cheese okay for the omelet?"

"No limburger. That stuff stinks worse than a double-dead skunk!"

"Stinks period. Got some bacon and shredded bruschetta." Dakota carried both packages to the counter.

"Gonna be an international omelet." Logan cracked the last egg into the bowl.

"How'd you get introduced?" Dakota took the bowl from Logan, added milk and started whisking the eggs.

"Not too different from you. She picked Earl up from the county supervisors' meetings often. Also, a couple of college classes."

"Me too. Grad school had me doing a lot of research." Dakota poured the eggs into the warm frying pan on the stove.

"We've both danced with her at the Sadie Hawkins events." Logan wheeled back to the table. "Guess we eat in the dining room. More space."

"Let's see what Cassandra wants." Dakota placed several strips of bacon into the microwave. After turning it on, he started washing and peeling potatoes.

"So we're both interested. She's shown an interest in us. What now?" Logan asked, placing napkins and silverware on the small kitchen table.

Dakota walked to the table after getting two mugs out and filling them with coffee. "We ask her what she wants. She knows some of our pack share mates."

"True. Maggie never hid her dual nature and they're best friends." Logan took a sip of coffee. Dakota watched him close his eyes. Man enjoyed a good cup of coffee.

"Oh, you coffee snob, you," Logan teased, his eyes still closed. "Chocolate amaretto and the dark roast."

Dakota smiled and nodded even though he knew Logan couldn't see him. "We're worth it. Besides, we supertasters deserve a taste of nirvana now and then."

Logan laughed as he opened his eyes. "Nirvana is good coffee and the smell of home cooking. Those eggs are gonna be good."

Dakota sipped his coffee twice before he stood. "Okay, you start crumbling bacon and mix it with some of the cheese. I'll get the home fries going."

Creaks and footsteps sounded overhead. Logan looked up as he took the bowl of cheese and bacon from Dakota. "Sounds like our lady is on her way down."

As Cassandra stepped into the living room, a delicious aroma greeted her. She inhaled again. Coffee—-fresh coffee tickled her nose. Another scent followed behind it. Chai Tea came and went as she made her way to the kitchen. A bouquet of spices and tantalizing fragrances welcomed her the closer she got. She caught glimpses of Dakota's back where the stove was. Logan came into sight, maneuvering around the kitchen in the wheelchair. She opened her mouth to speak as she neared the doorway. Closing her mouth, she spun around heading toward the window. Logan's statement—-"Our lady"—-it couldn't mean. . .could it?

Cassandra reached for the curtain covering part of the window. Taking a deep breath, she peered outside. Glancing across the yard even though her mind was elsewhere, her thoughts warped in directions faster than her heart could beat. Instead of the steady beat she knew, rapid staccatos moved through her upward to her ears. Calm had to prevail. Inhaling slowly, she focused on the scene outside. Though snow came up to windows, she could make out the house next door. If she turned to her left, she could see Dakota's pickup and into part of the truck's bed. Snow covered a good portion of it. She estimated ten to twelve inches lined the bed. To her right, drifts varied as she looked more toward the street and the bits and pieces she could make out of her neighbors' houses. Flakes fell larger than before, not at a solid rate. Could this be the lull the weather forecaster called for?

One last deep breath, she held it before turning back toward the kitchen. She'd made up her mind. What she overheard mattered. Letting it overwhelm her made no sense. The topic was between Dakota and Logan until they brought it up. Then a discussion could begin. Where her part in this was she didn't know yet. Both men interested her and caught her attention in many areas. Right now food and knowing the weather's next move took priority.

"Good morning," she called out, letting Dakota and Logan know she approached. If they continued their discussion, she wasn't eavesdropping and didn't want them to think she was. Dulce trotted ahead of her into the kitchen. Her shrill yip and tail wiggle said she knew the people.

"Morning," Dakota answered, turning from where he stood at the stove. He held a spatula in one hand and her large frying pan in the other. Delicious mixed aromas wafted toward her. Cheese, eggs, and bacon with a touch of extra spice, she suspected was one of the poblano chilies she picked up at the international market in Coeur d'Alene during her fall visit there.

"How'd you sleep?" Logan asked from where he sat buttering toast. Next to him sat one of her mugs with the string of a tea bag wrapped around the handle.

"Deeply for a storm that liked to whistle and blow." Cassandra moved toward the cabinet holding plates when she saw the kitchen table. Placemats, utensils, and napkins for three lay a top it. In the middle sat the carton of half and half and her sugar bowl. Either Dakota remembered where she kept things or they weren't averse to ferreting things out on their own. A quick shiver ran over her from her shoulders down her front and back. Crap, her nipples hardened like they announced where her psyche lingered. Couldn't it stay sated for a while longer? Maybe four to five hours more. She couldn't pluck at her top without drawing attention. How nonchalant could she appear? Acting wasn't one of her strong suits.

"I think we all slept sound," Dakota offered as he started toward the table. "Cassandra if you'll get the plates, I can dish this up." He hefted the pan up some before moving to the table. He stepped around Dulce.

"Plates coming up." Cassandra opened the cabinet, breathing deeply and offering a quick prayer the conversation hadn't gone straight over to what she overheard. She took three plates from the cabinet. As she turned, Logan reached toward the plates she held.

"I can use one for the toast." Logan pointed to the slices lying on a paper towel on the counter.

She set one on the counter and took another out. "No problem. I'd like some orange juice. Anyone else?"

"Sure," both Dakota and Logan answered.

"I'll get it in a moment." Cassandra placed the plates on the table. She retrieved the pitcher of juice from the refrigerator and filled three glasses. She carried those to the table while Dakota finished filling plates with eggs and potatoes. Logan wheeled over to the table, balancing the toast-filled plate on his lap.

Dakota refilled his and Logan's mugs with coffee. A whistle started indicating the electric kettle was hot. Dakota carried it and the mug with a tea bag in it to the table. "How full you want this?" He held the kettle over her mug.

"Two-thirds please." Cassandra sat down in the chair opposite where Logan sat. Dakota soon joined them. Dulce flopped on the floor closest to Cassandra.

Cassandra stirred sugar and half and half into her tea. She looked at Logan and Dakota both patiently waiting. Dakota never waited when they ate at the diner. What brought about this show of gentile manners? And Logan, well the only meals she shared with him were the buffet lines at the Sadie Hawkins events. They talked as they stood with other people, often holding their plates and eating at the same time. Two huge rocks tried making their way down her throat as she tried to swallow and smile. Cassandra laid her spoon on the napkin next to her plate. She sipped her tea. Hot, sweet, and creamy like she liked...

"Did the food turn out okay?" Dakota asked, smoothing his napkin across his lap. He looked across from him, smiled, and lifted his mug. "Here's to food, friends, and good conversation."

Cassandra returned his smile. It didn't reach her eyes. Her gaze darted back and forth from him to Logan. Something bothered her. He wondered if Logan noticed this. Another item for the list they needed to discuss. He'd have to figure it out later.

Dakota nudged Logan with his foot. Logan's grimace said he connected with the wrong one. Dakota quickly shrugged when Logan glanced at him, squinting to the point of glaring.

"Logan, are you all right?" Cassandra set her cup down and placed her hands on the table. She appeared ready to go to Logan's aid.

"My bad," Dakota blurted out, hoping Cassandra bought what he said next. "I didn't check before I moved my foot."

Logan nodded, shifting in his chair toward Cassandra. "I've done the same to Dakota sitting at the break room table."

Silence followed. Dakota picked up his fork and started eating. He chewed carefully, deciding what he could say next to get a conversation going. As if on cue, the grate on the screen door began to hum and a loud clapped of thunder sounded as snow began to rapidly fall.

"Great," Cassandra sighed, toying with her fork. "I'd hoped to get a path shoveled and the neighbors checked on before the storm hit."

Dakota laid his fork down. "Let's catch the news and weather while we eat."

He rose and walked over to where the clock radio sat on the counter. He checked the dial before turning it on. As he walked back to the table, the weather report came on.

"Good morning folks. The upper state is covered with snow. Some areas have three or more feet with another ten to twelve inches on the way. The stalled storm..." The announcer went on to local areas alphabetically. "Now Cauldron Falls, you folks are in between the last storm and the one that we're keeping an eye on up near the border."

"Great," Logan groaned, slumping down in the wheelchair.

"Hear him out," Dakota added, holding up his hand.

"A quick low is passing through stirring up more snow and creating thunder snow for the next hour. By noon, clearing will begin until later this evening. If you got outdoor chores to do, I suggest getting them done before sundown. You could get another twelve-plus inches over the next forty-eight hours."

Cassandra started eating again. She sipped her tea as she finished her omelet. "I eat fast. So go ahead while I think out loud here."

Dakota and Logan nodded. They resumed eating as she spoke. "Heat and lights will work even if power goes out thanks to the solar panels on the roof. There's plenty of wood in the basement if needed."

"Good," Dakota said after a few bites. "Hot water tank and pipes?"

"Insulated to withstand down to forty below. Granddad made sure the house would withstand a brutal winter. This place used to house the Beta-Xi Fraternity."

Dakota groaned, shaking his head. "And the land between here and the campus?"

"Dual custody. Granddad holds the deed. I'm on the title. College rents their portion from me." Cassandra sipped more of her tea, reaching down to pet Dulce.

Logan grinned as she glanced at him. "Well looks like your pricks are on your property. Gee Dakota, what are we gonna do about this?"

"Hmmm. Let me see. Local ordinances say lewdness is a ten-day jail sentence. Overt lewdness well that is in the eye of the beholder." Dakota sipped his coffee, grinning at her in between sips.

"And county ordinances. . ." Logan's voice trailed off.

"Your points are?" Cassandra reached for another piece of toast.

"Mrs. Robinson's vision isn't what it used to be. Everyone knows she needs her glasses to see clearly." Dakota glanced at Logan.

Cassandra took another bite of toast. These two were on a roll. She chewed and swallowed. "I see. Go on."

"With all that snow out there, who's to say what she actually saw. Evidence isn't exactly uncovered, now is it?" Logan smirked as he went back to eating.

"And," Dakota began, "Me and my prick ain't going out in that cold snow."

"Not my cock either," Logan declared.

Cassandra set her mug down. Mirth rose from deep inside her. Dakota and Logan's grins reminded her of the Cheshire cat from Alice in Wonderland. Her shoulders started moving first. Each time she looked at them, they smiled and went back to eating. One eek, then another escaped as she tried to keep from laughing.

"Give up darlin'," Dakota drawled in his best over-exaggerated twang. "You know you wanna."

"Yeah, what he said," Logan quipped, adding his own nasal high-pitched tone. "Teehee and no spitting please."

Peals of laughter escaped as she tried to cover her mouth with her hand. Dakota's chortles followed. Logan's chuckles mixed in shortly thereafter. Ten minutes passed before any of them could look at the other without merriment starting again.

Cassandra wiped her eyes as she spoke. "Oh my," she sighed. "That broke the ice."

As if the deities waited for the cue, a loud crack followed by thunder sounded. Dakota rushed to the kitchen window. Looking out he spoke. "Icicle is all."

"Wind will do that." Cassandra walked over to the microwave and put her mug in to warm it up. "Thank you for cooking Dakota. You too Logan."

Dakota started placing dishes in the sink. Logan gathered what he could put on his lap and wheeled to the sink as well. As the microwave dinged, Dakota spoke. "What do we do now?"

Cassandra looked at the window. Snow blew as the wind swirled more of it into sight. She noted the size of the flakes as she removed her mug from the microwave. At this rate, the snow would taper off soon. What did they do until then? Her quirky humor nibbled at her ready to erupt with cornball remarks that had nothing to do with the issue at hand.

But I might her psyche whispered. *How about a few hands of strip poker? Get everyone naked. Then see what happens!*

She quickly rolled her eyes, hoping Dakota and Logan hadn't seen her do it. She raised her mug and sipped. "Ugh, not warm enough."

Dakota walked over to her, took her mug and placed it back in the microwave.

CHAPTER SIX

'Thank you," Cassandra said, making her way to the sink. She opened the dishwasher, ready to place their dirty dishes inside.

"I'll dry if you wash," Dakota offered, taking the dishtowel she kept on the towel rack next to the hooks holding the potholders and other items she used when cooking.

"Sure." She closed the dishwasher. Ran hot water and detergent in the stoppered sink while she looked for the drain board she used from time to time. Taking it out from a large storage drawer, she glanced to where Logan sat watching her and Dakota. "Logan, is something bothering you?"

Logan wheeled to where he could see Cassandra and Dakota. He inhaled, placed his palm on his thigh, and spoke. "I want to say thank you to both of you."

Dakota leaned against the counter facing him as he dried a plate. "Welcome. You're family."

Cassandra glanced over her shoulder at him as she washed their utensils. She smiled as she spoke. "I'm glad I could help. Friends help friends."

"What if we were more?" Dakota opened the cabinet where Cassandra had gotten the plates earlier. He sat the dry ones inside, closing the cabinet as he reached for the third full coffee pot. He picked up a dry mug and filled it. "Logan, refill for you too?"

"Thanks. Better turn on the microwave. Reheat the tea." He rolled past Dakota and reached for the microwave. "Forty-five seconds good?"

"Yes, thank you." Cassandra turned away from him, rinsing the skillet.

Dakota poured the remainder of the pot into the mug close to him. After turning the coffeemaker off, he carried both mugs to the table. He spoke as he sat down. "The three of us have been friends for quite a while."

Logan joined Dakota at the table. "Cassandra, please join us?" He pulled out a chair for her between him and Dakota.

Cassandra dried her hands on the damp towel Dakota had used to dry the dishes. "One moment, please."

She moved past them, stepping into the laundry room. Why was she moving slowly? The timer dinged on the microwave as she reentered the kitchen. She took her mug from the microwave. She raised the mug to her and blew. Was her mug that warm? Or was this a stall tactic?

Logan looked at Dakota who watched Cassandra as well. Calling her on her actions might create problems. Dakota started to rise when she looked up. Dakota asked his question again as he sat back down. "What if we were more?"

"More what?" Cassandra asked, sitting down next to Dakota. Logan moved so all of them had ample room.

"More than friends," Logan answered.

"What?" Cassandra's mouth hung open.

Logan picked up his mug and drank. Telling Cassandra she could close her mouth probably would sound as idiotic as him thinking it. Dakota remained quiet. What was his reasoning?

Dakota turned so he faced Cassandra and could see Logan. Letting her recover from the shock. . .was it shock? Or more dismay? He wanted to wait to give her more time to react. Surprise didn't sit well with a lot of people.

Logan continued drinking his coffee even though his gaze met his more than once in the growing silence. Sitting drinking coffee sheepishly looking at each other between swallows made no sense either. Cassandra clutched her mug tightly. She'd sip then lowered the mug slightly. Was she hanging on to it for security? Maybe asking the next question was up to him. Dakota glanced at Logan who shook his head briefly, then saluted him with his mug before he sat it down on the table.

Dakota wet his lips and spoke. "Does this surprise you?"

Cassandra looked at him, drank from her mug, and sat the mug on the table. He could tell her breathing slowed. Her chest rose less agitatedly than it had after Logan's remark. Her eyes lingered on him longer with each glance at him and Logan. Where her thoughts went he didn't know. Getting her to talk might take a bit of prodding.

Dakota repeated his question. "Does this surprise you?"

Cassandra shook her head. "Some. But it caught me off guard."

"In what way?" Logan asked, placing his mug on the table. He pushed back from the table. "I need to use the bathroom."

"Half bath is past the stairs. You can get in with the wheelchair." Cassandra started to rise.

"I can find it. Go on with your conversation with Dakota." Logan wheeled out of the kitchen.

"So what caught you off-guard?" Dakota asked as Cassandra sat back down.

"Maybe strength of interest? Discussing it now? I can't say what exactly." Cassandra leaned back in her chair.

"I recently asked you out to dinner and a movie." Dakota leaned forward.

"We split the cost. I took that as we went as friends." Cassandra started to pick up her mug.

Dakota laid his hand on Cassandra's arm. "Sorry I wasn't clearer. Maybe you're feeling put upon?"

Cassandra set her mug down and covered Dakota's hand with hers. "Not put upon. You're interested. From his remarks so is Logan."

"Yes, I am," Logan called out, wheeling back into the kitchen. Dulce trotted in behind him. She walked over to the door and whined.

Cassandra rose, making her way to the door. "So you're both interested. I value our friendships. I don't want to choose one of you over the other or lose your friendship."

Dulce began pawing at the door, wiggling as she did. Cassandra opened the door enough to let her out. Dulce started out the door as a blast of wind pushed against the door. Dulce backed up, turned around and bolted toward the front room. Cassandra quickly shut the door. She peered out the window, sighing. Snow blew as the wind swirled more of it into sight. She noted the size of the flakes. Dulce needed to go out. Shoveling the walk and checking on her neighbors mattered. Cassandra turned back to where Dakota and Logan sat watching her. She spoke as she made her way to them. "Dulce isn't going to go out unless I put her out. That means a coat for her. Her dog yard needs shoveling."

"I think that means we table our discussion for now. Work calls." Dakota rose.

"I need thinking space. Busy work helps me think." Cassandra picked up her mug from the table and placed it in the sink. "I agree with more discussion later."

She paused near the laundry room door, glancing at Dakota and Logan. How domestic was Logan? She knew Dakota did a lot of the upkeep and cleaning at his office and home. The contracted cleaning service for the jail and sheriff's office talked about his pitching in more than once.

"Work?" Logan asked wheeling back to the table.

Dakota laughed. "Do chores sound better?"

Cassandra grinned as Dakota got closer. "Nothing onerous, I assure you. Shoveling snow, checking on the neighbors and laundry."

"Doesn't sound like I'm going to be much help." Logan slumped in his chair.

Let me see what there is," Cassandra said as Dakota moved past her.

"I'll pull my jeans on and meet you back here in ten minutes," Dakota said making his way into the laundry room. He came out holding a sweatshirt and jeans.

Cassandra moved past Dakota into the laundry room. The basket containing Dakota and Logan's clothes sat on top of the dryer. Her laundry filled the hamper sitting next to the washer. Washing their clothes together was more than she could handle right now. Letting either of them handle her undergarments much less see them probably labeled her prudish. So what. Comfort zones mattered. Right now, the edges of hers were frayed and unraveling. She'd take care of hers later. Getting Logan started on his and Dakota's laundry made more sense.

After all, men usually wore colors or whites. Logan could handle simple sorting into two or three loads along with the front loading washer and dryer. Folding might need more room. Dining room table offered that. It wasn't like she hadn't seen men's underwear. As she turned back toward the kitchen, a second thought poked her. *You haven't seen or handled theirs before.* She stepped back into the kitchen rubbing her wet palms down her jeans.

"Logan, there are two things you can help with." She moved to where he sat.

Logan looked up, smiling. "Okay. What you got for me?"

"How about your laundry? Dakota and I may be a while shoveling."

Logan blinked, looked down. She could see his chest rise and fall as he inhaled. Had he messed up his own laundry? Mixed colors and whites? Ended up with color-streaked underwear?

Cassandra reached toward Logan when he looked up and spoke. "With a bit of help, yes I can do the laundry."

"What help do you need?"

"Sorting instructions and preferred wash temps or cycles." Logan wheeled toward the laundry room. "Don't want to mess things up."

Cassandra pressed her lips together keeping her grin at bay. Logan tried to sound cheerful. She bet he dreaded doing laundry. Some men did. "Easy instructions for you. Whites in one load. Dark colors in another. Light colors usually can go in with the darks."

Cassandra stepped back into the laundry room taking the basket off the dryer, stacking it in two of hers sitting on the washer. She carried the baskets into the kitchen and stopped close to the table where Logan sat.

"Sounds easy enough. I've usually got one mixed load. Uniforms get dry cleaned." He took the baskets from her, separating the full one from the two empty ones.

"Use this basket for the whites." Cassandra held up a light blue basket. "Use the green one for colors. If anything stumps you, set it aside in the beige one."

"Thanks. Now the washer?" Logan set his basket on the table.

"I'll show you that when I come back down. Give me ten minutes." Cassandra trotted out of the kitchen with Dulce on her heels.

As Cassandra started up the stairs, Dakota met her halfway. He grinned and winked at her as he passed. He carried the towels he and Logan used the night before. The man was up to something. She'd worry about that later. Socks and her hikers took priority. Getting Dulce into her coat would take a few minutes, too. Her look at the snow and going rigid refusing to set foot out the door wasn't going to stop one stubborn pug from finding herself outside. Little did Dulce know a coat and a path were in her future. She could handle a brief tour outdoors. "I'll be back down in ten minutes," Cassandra called out as she reached the landing and continued upstairs toward her room.

Dakota continued into the kitchen dropping the towels on the table next to the basket Logan reached into. "I see you got your chores cut out for you."

"You could help, you know. Or are you going out in your socks?" Logan pointed at Dakota's foot.

"No, I'm putting my hikers on now." Dakota sat in the chair, pulling his hikers on. "Keep sorting. You'll make a stay-at-home husband yet."

"Smart mouth." Logan held up a multicolored shirt. "Separate or in with the colors."

Dakota tied his hikers. "That's okay. It's colorfast. I've washed it with darks or lights."

"Thanks. I think I've got this under control." Logan tossed socks and underwear into the blue basket.

"Appreciate you being good-natured about this. I'll try to get Cassandra back inside while I check on the neighbors and do their walks." Dakota started toward the door.

"Setting me up?" Logan tossed jeans and colored t-shirts into the green basket.

"Sorta. You need time with Cassandra as much as I do." Dakota slipped into his parka. He made his way back to the chair, combing his fingers through his hair as he did. He commented further as he braided his hair. "I've had more time with her than you."

"Sure. Did you express your interest recently?" Logan pulled the towels off the table into the empty basket he sat on the floor.

"Not directly. That is part of what we're going to discuss later." Dakota stood as Dulce ran into the kitchen.

"Come back you rascal. Your coat is going on and you're going out." Cassandra called out. She entered the kitchen holding a bright red bundle.

"Dulce's?" Dakota pointed at the bundle.

"Yes. She knows this means she's going out. And she hates the cold." Cassandra started toward Dulce only to have her run under the table.

"Some days, I swear I'd be better off with a cat." Cassandra leaned down, reaching for Dulce.

Dulce ran out the other side toward Logan. He leaned down, grabbing her collar. "Come here you. Be a good girl and hold still for me."

Dulce twisted and turned trying to work her way clear of Logan's grip. Dakota reached down scooping Dulce up. He sat her on Logan's lap. "Stay." He knew the words probably wouldn't work.

Cassandra handed Dulce's coat to him. "Pulls over her head like a sweater. There's openings for her front legs."

"What are you going to do?" Dakota asked, slipping his fingers under Dulce's collar.

"Get my coat and hat. There's snow to shovel." Cassandra turned back the way she came.

Dakota looked at Logan and nodded. Logan took ahold of Dulce's collar next to where he held it. Laying the coat on Logan's shoulder, Dakota spoke. "Let me go shovel a path for Dulce. You can help Logan with her coat. She'll probably sit still for you."

Dakota started for the back door, reaching into his parka pocket for the watch cap he kept stashed in it. Cowboy hats didn't keep heads warm in snowstorms. Cassandra's laugh stopped him. He turned to face her.

"Dulce staying still is like asking a snake to play dead." Cassandra stood with her hands on her hips staring at him as if he had purple hair. Not that he cared to repeat last Halloween's costume. It took six weeks to get the purple and green dye out of his hair.

Dakota shrugged. "I can clear a patch for her quickly. She isn't going to want to be out long."

Cassandra made her way back to where Logan sat holding Dulce on his lap while trying to pull the coat over her head. "Go on please. The shovels are in the shed at the back of the carport."

"Great. Give me about fifteen minutes. Then I'll get the squirm bug for her outing while you get ready." Dakota took a hold of the doorknob pausing, hoping Cassandra went along with his idea. Giving Logan time with her mattered, after all, they needed to bond as couples and a trio. His and Logan's friendship began during their high school years. Their comfortableness with each other was solid. He glanced back at Logan and Cassandra and smiled. Opening the door, he stepped outside shutting the door behind him.

Cassandra reached for the coat Logan tried to pull over Dulce's head. "Hold her and I'll get it. She doesn't like her head covered."

Logan let go of the bunched-up coat. "She is a live wire."

"She's a firecracker at times. Last summer she chased Chuy down the street because he took her ball." Cassandra reached through the coat's opening and placed a hand on Dulce's head holding her as still as she could. After the second tug, the coat slipped over Dulce's head. As if on cue, Dulce stopped wriggling.

"I bet that was a sight. Chuy can run fast. Did Dulce catch him?" Logan patted Dulce as Cassandra finished putting the coat on her.

"Yes and no. Chuy kept dropping the ball. Third time he dropped the ball, Dulce caught up with him. Watching the two of them go head over heels had Mrs. Abernathy and me laughing so hard we wiped tears."

Logan snickered. "I bet Dulce grabbed her ball and ran." He petted Dulce who squirmed whenever she heard her name.

"I wish she had. Mrs. Tinders' german shepherd ran up and grabbed the ball. Took off toward their yard and leaped the fence." Cassandra started toward the door.

"Did you get the ball back?" Logan maneuvered the wheelchair so he could see Cassandra.

"No. Good thing too. The ball ended up buried somewhere in the Tinders backyard. Last spring, once Mr. Tinders rototilled for the garden, several missing items showed up." Cassandra picked up her coat. "I'm going to check on Dakota."

"Give him time. If he doesn't respond soon, then check." Logan looked at the clock on the wall near the stove. "Say ten minutes?"

Cassandra hung her coat back on the peg coat rack and crossed over to him. She glanced toward the door twice. "I guess Dakota will let us know when he's ready for Dulce."

Logan pointed to Dulce. "Can I put her down?"

"Yes, she knows she's going out."

Logan put Dulce down on the floor.

"It's easier to talk when you're sitting down. You know my eye level." Logan wheeled back to the table, pulling out a chair close to him for Cassandra. He patted the chair. "Please," he added.

Cassandra glanced at the door again before nodding and sitting down. "All right."

"I'd wanted to talk to you about. . ." Logan let his words die off, hoping to get Cassandra's attention.

CHAPTER SEVEN

Logan leaned forward interlacing his fingers with Cassandra's. He raised her hand to his lips and kissed her knuckles. "You know I'm interested in you."

"Yes, I do."

"How do you feel about that?" Logan let go of Cassandra's hand. Cassandra looked away and then back at him, though her eyes didn't meet his. Her breathing changed the longer he watched her. "I'm—-"

Cassandra interrupted him. "I'm—well—-" She wiped her hand down her jeans. Closed her eyes and pressed her lips together.

Logan laid his hand on her wrist. "Are you intrigued?"

Cassandra nodded, fanning herself. She looked to the door. "All of this boggles my mind. Intrigue doesn't compute right now. Sorry."

She stood moving away. She walked over to one of the baskets of clothes and picked it up. She stood still as if in thought. Logan rolled away from the table ready to go around her when she turned. "Let's get this laundry started. I'll show you how the washer works."

Logan followed, enjoying the view. Cassandra walked with a natural flow to her hips moving as she pleased. There was no exaggerated tightness to her ass or a sway that came across as a put-on move. A woman comfortable in her own skin and sexuality sparked him, ignited his interest and chemistry in ways that sometimes defied words or thought. Watching Cassandra did this. He could sit and watch her without commenting. Her natural sexiness shined. She moved with an easiness about her that said 'I'm me and that's okay.' Her thoughtfulness and caring about people ranked high with him. He took one last look as he reached the laundry room doorway. As his gaze reached Cassandra's shoulders and neck, he caught her watching him. He smiled, shrugged and reached for the empty basket she held. "Sorry, I got lost in my thoughts."

"It's okay. I do that too from time to time." Cassandra startled, looking down to where his hand touched hers.

"Sorry," Logan started to draw his hand back.

"It's okay. Really." Cassandra's gaze met his. Her gaze lingered a bit and looked away.

Logan tapped the basket. "I can hold this while you show me what to do."

"That would make things easy." Cassandra set the basket on Logan's lap. She turned to the shelves at the rear of the laundry room, speaking as she did.

"One pod per load." She held up the container, making sure Logan got a good look.

Logan nodded. "Got it."

"Has detergent and softener in it." She opened the washer door. "You can add a boost pod if you need stains lifted or a bit of color-safe bleach." She held up a second pod.

"With Dakota's and my stuff, wouldn't hurt." Logan wheeled closer. "What about water temp?"

"Set already. Warm wash. Cold rinse." Cassandra tossed the second pod into the washer and reached for the basket.

"Sounds easy enough." Logan handed her the basket. His fingers brushed over hers. Another spark sizzled over her wrist and laved its way across her palm before dancing into the air. She blinked twice, staring hard where their hands met. Was that a glow? A coral flicker? She looked away, inhaling. Tendrils of heat danced around her field of vision casting flickers of coral in between specks of yellow and white. As she exhaled, her vision cleared. She glanced at Logan as he spoke.

"Damn. Laundry is easy. Why didn't I get it before?" Logan smiled, reaching for the washer door.

"Knowing the basics helps. Dakota learned a few things, too. Ask him about pink briefs." Cassandra loaded the clothes into the washer.

"Pink?" Logan chuckled. "Too much bleach?"

"Tried a mixed load of colors and whites." Cassandra shut the door. "New sheets and shirts decided to liven up his whites."

"Rule number one, don't wash new clothes with whites. Got it." Logan pointed to the washer. "Start button?"

"Large gray one." Cassandra pushed it.

"What about these?" Logan reached toward the hamper behind her.

"I'll take care of those." Cassandra started to move between the hamper and Logan.

"I can sort them for you." He took her hand. Another bolt of heat flickered over her hand and wrist. This one didn't stop there. It sizzled and burned its way up her arm, coiling around her upper arm like a band ready to snake its way over the rest of her, prepared to strike at any moment. She swallowed hard. Pulling her hand away wasn't an option. Logan hadn't made a move on her since he kissed her hand. Jerking away from him would send a rejection message. One she didn't want to deliver or mean. She took a breath, then another. Halfway through her third, she pressed her lips together. No, it couldn't be. Could it?

Shapeshifter subtle marking can happen at any time. Maggie's voice echoed through her mind. Logan a shapeshifter? He never said anything. Was Dakota one too? He'd touched her several times and nothing like this had...oh, shit! Her erotic dreams about him started after his first dance with her two Sadie Hawkins events back. Marked? Claimed? Or natural chemistry? She tried swallowing again. A dry mouth and throat didn't aid speaking.

"Thanks for offering." Cassandra waved her hands. "I'm finicky about my clothes."

Logan backed up. "Understood. Probably why my mother and sisters insisted dad and I didn't do laundry."

Cassandra snickered. "Granddad said more than once straight forward wash was okay. Reading too many labels got nothing done."

"Got a point." Logan wheeled part way out of the laundry room.

"He does darks, sheets, and towels. Leaves the rest for Gram and me." Cassandra paused by the dryer. "Dryer is set on medium heat and sensor."

"Load it and push start, right?" Logan offered.

"Right. It buzzes when done like the washer." Cassandra waited until Logan was back in the kitchen before she continued. "You can fold clothes on the dining room table."

"Thanks. Is it okay to leave the basket on the table?" Logan wheeled to the middle of the kitchen, turned and faced her.

"Sure. We'll—-" The click of the door opening interrupted Cassandra.

"Okay you squirm bug. Time to go." Dakota spoke as he opened the door.

Dulce barked and started toward the living room, moving as fast as she could. Cassandra caught the blur of red as Dulce raced under the table.

Logan rolled forward, chuckling. "Gonna help Dakota corral Dulce."

"She's fast when she wants to be." Cassandra moved around the table, picking up speed as she did.

Dakotah pushed the door to as he entered the kitchen. "What's with her?" he asked, crossing to Cassandra and Logan. He countered his steps to theirs, making sure he stayed behind Dulce, out of her line of vision.

"Cold," Cassandra replied. "Told Granddad, a southern-born dog don't like cold."

"Neither do southern wolves I'm told." Dakota grinned as Cassandra shook her head. "Dogs and wolves are related. Learned that in college biology."

"More likely high school," Logan quipped, rolling past the table.

"Probably both," Dakota countered, moving up next to Cassandra.

The trio formed a semi-circle around Dulce. Step-by-step they herded her backward toward the wall between the end of the counter and the door where Logan's crutches leaned against the wall.

"Got you," Dakota claimed, bending over to scoop up Dulce as she bolted toward him.

Dakota faced Cassandra with Dulce under one arm. "Ready for shovel duty?"

Dakota tightened his hold on Dulce. "You're going out. Like it or not." He patted Dulce's head.

"Yes, gotta get my coat." Cassandra moved around Dakota. She pulled on her coat and faced Logan. "Dryer timer will show forty-five minutes."

"Got it." Logan pointed at Dakota and Dulce. "Knock when you're ready to let Dulce in."

"I will. She may not want her coat off by then." Dakota turned toward the door. "I'll be outside."

Cassandra wrapped her scarf around her neck. "There's an afghan on the couch. You can wrap up in it when you open the door."

Logan chafed his arms as Dakota opened the door. A blast of wind buffeted its way around the door, reaching across the kitchen as if it wanted Logan.

"Thanks. I may need it," Logan replied, moving away from the door

"Come on, Dulce," Dakota spoke, making his way out the door. "Sooner you get done, the faster you get in."

"Yeah," Logan replied.

Cassandra didn't look back as she opened the door. "I'll check on you in a while," she called out, exiting.

Logan shook his head as he heard the door firmly shut. He bet Cassandra's thoughts were on Dakota and shoveling.

Logan glanced at his watch. 12:30 PM. Four and a half hours until nightfall. How hard the next storm hit them remained unknown. He rolled to where his crutches stood, propped against the wall near the counter. Placing both hands on the counter, he braced himself, raising on one foot.

"Oh man, my ass is numb!' He chuckled at his tone. The whine and pitch matched his ten-year-old nephew's drone as he complained about sitting in the car on a trip to his grandparents. Logan bet he mimicked him to a tee.

He winced as he placed one crutch under each arm. Muscles screamed in places he didn't think he could ache. Standing was better than a numb ass. Crutch, hop, crutch, hop. Eight weeks—-eight lousy weeks until he could do anything without a blasted chaperone. Independence was a sweet dream with goal scribbled next to it on his list of future to-do items.

"Praise Lupa," he muttered, continuing his crutch hop shuffle across the kitchen.

"Full moon marked, I ain't." He chuckled through clenched teeth.

Another crutch hop step and. . .a thump sounded.

"Fuck that hurts," he groaned. Sucking in air, he leaned against the door jam, glaring down at his good foot. The slipper he wore gapped on the sides. A white crew sock covered his foot up to his ankle. The sock's mate covered the ace bandage wrapped around his sprained ankle.

Pain raced up his calf, around his knee as muscles spasmed, threatening to lay him out like a limp rubber chicken. He glanced at the washer's timer noting twenty minutes remained. The dryer loaded from the front as well. Good, 'cuz he was getting back in the wheelchair. His ass could numb up all it wanted. If he fell, there went both ankles. Maybe his leg too. Not happening. Shift and healing missed his species.

Dakota called it the evolutionary generational split. Logan stuck out his tongue and blew a raspberry cheer. Didn't matter what science named or described it. He didn't care how detailed Dakota got in his explanation. Either of them could shift and their injuries remained. Good old-fashioned healing applied to their branches of shapeshifters.

Logan plopped into the wheelchair. He leaned his crutches against the wall. Wincing again, he rubbed his good leg up and down his calf. No sore spot except when he moved his toes. As he ran his fingers over his ankle, no pain occurred. Down over his foot, he carefully rubbed. No ouch rang out. Pulling off the slipper and sock, he examined his toes and foot. Two red spots stood out on his big toe. He flexed his toes. A twinge came and went. He pulled the sock back on and slipped his foot into the slipper. Leaning back in the chair, he sighed, letting go the breath he held.

Looking at the kitchen clock, he grinned. Ten minutes until the washer buzzed. Enough time to retrieve a magazine from the front room coffee table and be ready to put the clothes in the dryer. By the time he rolled back into the kitchen, the washer's buzzer sounded. Logan tossed the magazine on the kitchen table, lifted the basket of light colors onto his lap, and made his way into the laundry room. The washer buzzed again.

"Yeah, I hear ya." Logan snickered, voicing his next thought aloud. "Would tell ya hold your drawers on, but you ain't got none to hold, much less on."

He opened the washer and dryer doors. He shook out pieces as he pulled them out of the washer. "Mom would be proud of me. She always said shake 'em out. Helps them dry better."

Smiling at his banter, Logan continued shaking until all the clothes were in the dryer. He pushed start, noting the time. Next, he tossed in the pods like Cassandra showed him. "Lupa, this is easy!" He rolled his eyes, hearing his mother's chastisements about learning basic housekeeping chores. "Mom, I owe you next time I visit."

Knowing his mother, she'd probably extract lunch at her favorite restaurant in Coeur d'Alene plus a visit with his sisters and their matchmaking banter. Also, his mom's hints at more grandkids. His older brother needed to move back so Mom could pester him, too. Nothing wrong with kids. They needed parents who had time for them. Given his current work schedule and lack of staff, home life consisted of work, eat, sleep and work more. Had Dakota heard from the state on their joint request for funds and personnel? Logan made a mental note to talk to Dakota about it later.

Logan tossed the items in the basket in the washer, closed the door, and noted the amount of time on both timers. Rolling back into the kitchen, he glanced toward the window wondering if he should check on Dakota and Cassandra. He knew one thing. He wasn't opening the door without the afghan from the living room wrapped around him. The wind wasn't tickling him again. He'd had enough of its icy amusement last night.

He made his way out of the kitchen into the dining area. The sun broke through the clouds as he passed the window. Dakota's shadow cast upon the window as he moved toward the carport from the driveway. Logan couldn't make out what Dakota said. Muffled words faded as Dakota moved back under the carport. Logan grabbed the afghan off the back of the couch and turned around. He wrapped the afghan loosely around him before heading back to the kitchen. When the door opened, he'd be ready.

Meanwhile, catching up on the latest entertainment news out of Hollywood awaited him. Reading Hollywood tabloids filled time. It wasn't like he needed distracted concentration. Laundry required some mental attention. Logan snickered and turned to the table of contents, skimming to see what caught his attention.

CHAPTER EIGHT

Cassandra pulled the brim of her knitted hat lower. Wind swirled loose snow around her. Dakota stood at the back edge of the patio latching the gate of Dulce's dog yard. The scamp peered out from her doghouse. Cassandra noted the area beyond the doghouse. Evidence of Dulce answering nature's call marked the area Dakota had cleared inside the dog yard.

"Thanks," Cassandra said, moving closer to Dakota.

"You're welcome. Dulce deserves TLC too." Dakota turned toward the tool shed that shared the back portion of the carport. "She reminds me of Rocko."

"Rocko?" Cassandra asked, opening the shed door.

"Family dog. He loved to dig." Dakota held the door open.

"Mud and dirt everywhere, I bet." Cassandra entered the shed.

"Bunches. Loved to roll in anything stinky he could find." Dakota continued as she exited the shed. "Rocko loved his bubble baths too."

"Bubble baths? A dog?" Cassandra handed Dakota another snow shovel.

"Only way we could get him near soap and water was bubbles." Dakota smiled, shaking his head. "Give Rocko a bubble to chase and he'd get wet. Soaped down too."

Cassandra laughed. "So his TLC was a bubble bath chase."

"Yup. Crazy dog." Dakota started toward the end of the carport leading to the street.

Cassandra joined him at the edge of the carport. The partial path he'd hastily shoveled led away from the house toward the street devoid of cars. Dakota shielded his eyes as he glanced at the sky. Bright patches of blue dotted the cloud-filled overhead. Sunbeams broke through creating polka dots on the snow here and there.

"Nice lull. Damn cold too." Dakota stomped his feet.

"Definitely." Cassandra stepped out from under the carport. "Sure is quiet."

"Kinda nice for a change." Dakota touched her shoulder. "Might be easier if we worked together."

"What you got in mind?" Cassandra leaned on the handle of her shovel.

Dakota walked over to where he'd left his shovel in a drift near the chain link fence separating the two properties. "A couple of paths. One on each side of the driveway."

"Clear off enough of the driveway apron to get in and out if needed?" Cassandra picked up her shovel.

"Not worth it at this point. Too much work with the next storm coming." Dakota pointed to the single wide path close to the fence line. "Path to the Millers started. I saw Dave Timber out earlier."

"Good. His son arrived midweek with his wife and kids. Bet they're going stir crazy." Cassandra smiled as she faced Dakota.

"There was a snowball battle going on in between shoveling." Dakota grinned, adding. "The dog got in on it too."

"Nuba loves playing catch. Frisbee agility." Cassandra started widening Dakota's path. She glanced over her shoulder and stopped. Dakota stood behind her, gazing at her, grinning. "Sounds like we don't need to check on the Timbers."

"No," Dakota replied, moving up beside her. "Dave waved and called out they're okay."

"Good." Cassandra tossed two more shovels full of snow onto the drift burying the fence. Dakota kept pace alongside her doing nothing more than watching her for several shovels full. "What are you doing?"

"Thinking how to make this easier. Go faster."

"Oh?" Cassandra leaned on her shovel, arched an eyebrow, and opened her mouth to say more.

"Yes. Let's meet in the middle. It'll go faster." Dakota pointed to the end of the driveway. "I'll start from there."

"Makes sense." Cassandra started to scoop up another shovel full. Dakota hesitated. She faced him. "What?"

"This." Dakota leaned in, brushed his lips over hers, and pulled back. "A bit of inspiration." He turned and sauntered down the drive whistling.

Cassandra blinked, stared, and blinked again as Dakota walked away. If she didn't know better, she'd swear he swung his hips back and forth tempting her to gawk at him even more. Shit, did he know how often she gave his firm ass the once over? This morning he gave her an eye full as he helped Logan. He couldn't know, could he? There was that question again. What did or could either Dakota or Logan know. Made no sense except warmth started at her cheeks and spread down her neck. He called his act inspiration? Kissing her to inspire what? Her psyche flicked back to the images burned into it from this morning. She'd gotten an eyeful for sure. One that she wasn't going to forget or wanted to.

She gripped the shovel handle and skimmed the top layer off the drive section closest to her. The weather report called for more blowing and snowfall. Where they shoveled could be covered again come morning. Clearing paths and making sure they could get out of the drive were their best options. Cassandra cleared three sections of the drive by the time she reached Dakota. She looked up, nodding. "Sorry. Mind elsewhere as I shoveled. I can clear more."

"Don't sweat it. Need is to clear out behind the truck and put down some melt. Should keep the worst of it from icing over with the next storm." Dakota leaned his shovel against the house. "I can finish up. You and Dulce go on inside."

Cassandra shook her head. "I can put the meltdown."

Dakota closed the space between them. "Darlin'," he began, reaching for her shovel. "Independence is great. You got help. Accept it. Please?"

Cassandra looked down. Dakota's feet came into view. He'd moved closer. She tipped her head back, his gaze meeting hers. He smiled and placed his hand on the shovel handle slightly below hers. He'd offered help without pushing it further. Maybe he got her need for independence. Some men didn't. She'd been on her own until her grandparents invited her to move in with them. Since her parents retired to Florida, she'd lived alone and did as she pleased. During the short time she'd lived with her grandparents, she hadn't gotten used to having others around. With their announcement they were traveling to decide where they wanted to retire; she was on her own again. Help wasn't a luxury. Her neighbors and friends freely offered theirs and took her up on hers. Why not take Dakota up on his?

She let go of the shovel. "Sure. I can set up Dulce's faux grass pads and pen on the sun porch while you finish up."

Dakota leaned the shovel against the house. "Okay. First, put Dulce inside. I'm sure Logan can use the company."

Cassandra laughed. "You mean the contest of if she'll let him get near her to get her coat off."

"That too." Dakota grabbed his shovel and turned, adding, "At least he'll get some exercise wheeling around after her."

Cassandra smirked as she walked to the dog yard. Dulce came running to the gate before it opened. Cassandra opened the gate and leaned down. She scooped Dulce up under one arm and started toward the house. Dakota met her at the steps.

"I've got the area behind the truck cleared. Where's the faux grass pads?" Dakota leaned his shovel against the house next to hers.

"Just inside the shed. The bag of melt is next to them." Cassandra reached for the doorknob as Dakota stepped away from her. "Thanks for helping out. I appreciate it."

Dakota nodded as he walked away. "Glad to. It's part of being here. Now put Dulce inside. That wind is blowing harder and colder."

Cassandra opened the kitchen door long enough to sit Dulce inside. "We're almost done out here, Logan."

"Second load in. First one is drying," Logan called out.

"Great. We'll be in shortly." Cassandra pulled the door shut.

Dakota laid the faux grass pads on the steps. "Go on in. I can finish up here," Dakota said, walking back to the shed.

Cassandra pressed her lips together. Part of her wanted to check again if Dakota needed help. She could see there wasn't anything more to do. The wind already blew snow back over where they'd shoveled. For now, they'd done the best they could. Watching and waiting until the second storm passed sounded rather boring and dull. If the two storms mixed, they were in for snowmageddon—a blizzard with a two-fold punch and staying power. Digging out would take everyone's help. She started to reach for the shovels when Dakota called out. "Leave them there. Easier to get to when we need them."

"True," she replied, stomping her feet to work off the worst of the snow. Cassandra picked up the faux grass pads off the steps and entered the house. As she closed the door, she glanced over her shoulder again. Dakota was wrestling a bag of melt out of the shed and dragging it toward the carport. Going through the storm alone was one thing. Counting on herself to do it all. With Dakota and Logan here, she didn't. When the storm was over, she didn't think things were going to be the same.

Logan pulled the afghan tighter around him as the kitchen exterior door opened. The wind raced in, blowing snow and cold through the open door right at him. He sat still, bracing himself for the on-slot of the icy fingers winter loved to dance across uncovered flesh. Except the only thing uncovered were his hand and face. He knew better than to taunt nature. No supernatural being did that and took it lightly. Nature's force was part of them. Their wild side embraced most of their animal side's traits. The full moon a week away would test quite a few shifters' resilience. Could they resist the draw of the moon and not shift? He'd resisted in the past. Taken time to prepare mentally and physically as well as his psyche. The lure and call aroused his baser nature, the urge to mate. This moon's allure would be different. He didn't want either he or Dakota wrestling with a case of blue balls and unsatisfied male hormones battling each other.

Dulce raced toward him. She stopped close to him, pawed the afghan and yipped. Logan chuckled. She wanted him to share, to share the afghan. He leaned down, hand out reaching toward Dulce. "Sure I'll share with you scamp. Let's get your coat off too."

Dulce backed up. Logan wheeled forward. Dulce backed up again. He rolled closer. "Look, I got the afghan. You want it. So do you let me get your coat off or. . ."

He turned and started to roll away from Dulce. She barked, yipped and barked again. He ignored her and kept moving back toward the kitchen table. As he reached the table, he glanced over his shoulder. Dulce followed him, her curly tail wagging as best it could.

"Oh, you ready to be nice?" Logan asked, turning around. Dulce yipped and got closer. He leaned down, sliding his hand down his leg this time.

Dulce walked right up to him. Logan looked around as he quickly slid his arm under Dulce and lifted. She didn't squirm or bark. He sat her on his lap, taking hold of her collar. She looked up at him with her brown eyes as if to say, get the coat off. Logan chuckled and began working the coat off Dulce. As soon as he had it off her, she started digging at the afghan, nosing what she could into a ball in his lap.

"Hey, just lay down. I want some too." Logan reached down to pull part of the afghan over Dulce.

The exterior door opened again. Cassandra entered. "She probably wants the whole thing. She burrows under the afghan every chance she gets when I let her up on the couch."

"Great colors. Nice pattern. She's got good taste like her owner." Logan wrapped Dulce in part of the afghan and wheeled toward Cassandra.

"I guess a thank you is needed." Cassandra took off her coat and hung it on the coat pegs behind the exterior door.

She noticed Logan's smile as she turned. "Sorry if I'm slow on the uptake."

"Let's get something straight, please." Logan held out Dulce's coat to her. "Manners are okay. Expecting perfection isn't."

Cassandra took Dulce's coat, shook it out, and hung it next to her coat. She noted the bits of ice that clung to both her coat and Dulce's. Dakota was still out in the cold and blowing wind. How much more could he take?

"Hey, what you thinking?" Logan asked, waving his hand up and down.

"Wondering how much more Dakota can take out in the wind and cold." Cassandra walked over to the table, pulled out a chair and sat down. "You're in front of me and I need to pay attention to you. My bad. I'm sorry."

'It's okay to a point." Logan started to wheel away from her.

"Wait," Cassandra began, reaching out toward Logan. "New territory. You're both here. In front of me."

Logan chuckled. "Yeah. In some aspects for us too. How about you and I focus on us for now?"

Cassandra looked away. The difference was now. There wasn't a getting used to it period by itself. Now was both. Time to embrace what was in front of her. She took a deep breath, held it, and slowly exhaled.

"Logan," she began, facing him. "I agree. We've bonded as friends. Maybe we're looking at is there more?"

Logan wheeled up to her, taking her hand as he spoke. "I sure am. Have been for a while."

Cassandra looked down, back up at Logan and back at their entwined hands. Another image flashed through her mind and quickly faded. She blinked, tried to bring the image back, and failed. Her mind wasn't going to let her focus on anything but Logan. Okay, focus she would. She looked up, waiting until Logan's gaze met hers.

"Good. You both intrigue me." Cassandra raised her and Logan's joined hands up to eye level. "This feels right. It feels good. There's something I wonder about."

"What is it?" Logan asked, slowly pulling his hand away.

"How much have you and Dakota talked about this?' Cassandra laid her hand on the table. "This sharing thing."

Logan sighed. How much did he say without Dakota present? This was one of those he and Dakota needed to be present items they talked about. *Shit!* He had to answer or Cassandra would think he was avoiding her question. Trust was a vital piece in creating a solid connection between the three of them. The cornerstone foundation piece that allowed them to build upon. Damn, he hated being cornered. Not that Cassandra had cornered him intentionally.

Logan turned the wheelchair until he could easily see Cassandra and watch her body language. Her nonverbal energy signature would come through. Reading auras wasn't his strong suit. He caught the intense colors flashing around the outer edges of her silhouette. Reds, yellows, and bursts of blue flashed at the outer edges of his vision. He hoped his answer sufficed, rang true for her, and sounded plausible. He wished he and Dakota had talked more. "Well," Logan began, not looking away. "We've talked. Different shifts. Different jobs. Not always easy to get together. Why do you ask?"

"Trying to understand. Maggie's talked about how the matchmakers finally came around to accepting that triads and quads are feasible." Cassandra nodded as she continued speaking.

"Are you interested in a triad?" Logan asked, closing the space between them.

CHAPTER NINE

Logan stopped as the wheelchair touched the chair Cassandra sat in. Closeness was one thing. Leaving enough space for Cassandra to feel safe and remain at ease was a vital part of keeping their communication flowing. He laid his hand on the table and repeated his question. "Are you interested in a triad?'

Dulce snuggled deeper into the afghan covering her on his lap. Cassandra reached out and petted Dulce as she responded. "I've talked with a few of the ones that are in the neighborhood. Even met some of the kids from others in town who attend the university. Seem like normal folks."

Logan noted the slight shake of her head. "Why are you shaking your head?"

"Normal for Cauldron Falls has quite a few definitions. The norm around here could be shape shifters, hybrid-a mix between two species like human and shape shifter." Cassandra leaned back in her chair.

"That is true. There are the prejudiced ones, too. We all seem to get along. I often wonder how we all do it." Logan grinned. "I agree. Makes life interesting keeping up with all the combinations. I'm glad xenobiology wasn't my undergrad major."

"I've read a little on it when the text and reference books on the subject first came into the library. My intrigue stopped when my mind and eyes glazed over with all the scientific terms and detailed facts." Cassandra laid her hand near his. "So you're interested in me. How so?"

He blinked. Talk about being caught with his mind elsewhere. Thoughts of Cassandra nude—cuddling with him under the afghan—caught his attention, drawing his attention away from what she said. Logan moved his hand closer to Cassandra's until his fingers touched hers.

"My interest is multifaceted. I like what I see in many aspects." Logan pressed his lips together, trying to not smirk at his inane answer. There were many things about Cassandra that intrigued him, caught his attention, and checked off several items on his ideal mate list. But as Dakota had pointed out more than once. Ideal wasn't always the best option. A mate that could keep up with both of them topped his and Dakota's mutual list.

"Explain, please." Cassandra watched him intently. How much did she know about him or Dakota?

"You're kind. Treat people with dignity and respect. You're lovely to look at. I find you captivating. Your sense of humor, intellect, and the whole package." Logan leaned forward, laying his other hand on Cassandra's arm. "Does that make sense?"

"To a point. That's the exterior package. What do you know of me inside?" Cassandra patted his hand and pulled back. "There's more to a person than what you see glimpses of."

Logan set Dulce on the floor. He inhaled slowly, considering his response. What Cassandra said made sense. They dated a couple of times. Interacted at official events and . . .how did he explain he watched her interact with others like when he was at the library doing research. Patrolling and making sure the campus and neighborhood were safe. Keeping Cauldron Falls, Sylvan Valley and the university safe meant keeping an eye and ear on things.

"I agree with you. Dakota's and my job is to serve and protect. We notice what is going on around us. As leaders, we get information on people, places and our preternatural residents. Do I know all about you? No, but I would like to." Logan rolled the wheelchair back from the table and started toward the laundry room as the dryer timer buzzed.

Cassandra followed Logan partway to the laundry room. "How does Dakota feel about this?"

"About what?" Dakota asked, closing the outside door behind him.

Cassandra faced Dakota. Logan backed out of the laundry room and turned around.

"Cassandra and I are talking about how well we know each other." Logan wheeled back to the table. "I asked her if she was interested in a triad."

Dakota shrugged out of his parka and hung it on a coat peg next to Cassandra's. "Two loaded questions. Ones that need discussing or you wouldn't have asked them."

Dakota leaned down and unlaced his hikers. "Cassandra, did I leave my slippers in here?"

"They're in the living room. I'll get them." Cassandra quickly exited the kitchen.

Dakota sat in the chair next to Logan. "What's with the triad topic? I thought we agreed to wait to discuss it."

"Cassandra sorta brought it up. She mentioned Maggie, and she talked about quads and triad pair bondings. I asked her if she was interested in a triad. Didn't say you and I in particular."

Dakota nodded as he pulled his hikers off. "Okay. So what did she say?"

"We both intrigue her. She asked if we'd discussed sharing and that we're both interested in her. I said we've talked. Didn't say specifics." Logan glanced toward the living room doorway.

Dakota leaned back in the chair. "Doesn't sound like you said anything wrong. Let's wait a few before we bring up the topic. I need a cup of coffee and something to eat. Shoveling snow worked off my breakfast."

Logan wheeled toward the laundry room. "Sure. I need to get the clothes out of the dryer and the batch in the washer drying."

"I'll get the coffee maker going. And check the fridge for lunch fixings." Dakota walked to the living room entrance. Cassandra sat on the couch, leafing through a magazine. He exited the kitchen and crouched down in front of her. Cassandra looked up.

"Are you okay?" Dakota held out his hand. "Why didn't you come back into the kitchen?"

"Didn't want to interrupt your and Logan's conversation. Heard my name and decided that I needed some space to think." Cassandra closed the magazine and laid it on the coffee table.

"Think about what?" Dakota sat down beside Cassandra. "If Logan or I said something wrong, we need to know."

"Neither of you said anything wrong." Cassandra handed Dakota his slippers. "You're both interested in me. You're not arguing about it. I've never had two guys interested in me at the same time. Much less one as enthusiastically as either of you are."

Dakota slipped his feet into the slippers and leaned forward. "Might sound kinda crass if I said darlin' you're worth it."

Cassandra snickered. "Thanks for the compliment. I don't have a runway model's figure. Nor am I a size eight. I'm chunky."

Dakota laid his hand on Cassandra's knee. "You got curves, love. Lady curves that I find very appealing. Runway models are too damn boney. I've had too many bruises from getting amorous with them if you know what I mean."

Cassandra snorted, shaking a finger at Dakota. "I think that is a bit of TMI."

"Nah." Dakota stood, offering Cassandra his hand. "Just a bit of getting to know me more. You already know I've got a scampish sense of humor that mixes with my ironical one at times."

"Oh, do I. Like the time you bluffed Granddad and his poker club into believing you had a full house. You played that one straight-faced and won the hundred dollar pot that night." Cassandra clasped Dakota's hand and stood up.

"The best part was the look on their faces as I doled the winnings back out to them and thanked them for a great game as I walked out." Dakota chortled.

"That must be the game I missed," Logan said, wheeling into the dining room, full clothes basket on his lap. "They talked about it for months. Every now and then, it comes up as a reminder of why you don't want to invite Sheriff Knox to play poker."

"Nothing wrong with a bit of a reputation." Dakota grinned. "How about some lunch? I could use a cup of coffee. Tea Cassandra?"

"No. Water for me. There's more soup I can warm up. Make some toast and cheese sandwiches?" Cassandra moved around Dakota.

"Teamwork on making lunch. Then we can fold laundry and talk about the dynamite word." Dakota took the basket off Logan's lap and set it on the dining room table.

"I'm game." Logan turned his chair around and moved toward the kitchen.

"Dynamite word?" Cassandra asked, pausing at the kitchen doorway.

"Topic that can ignite a conversation or blow up." Dakota entered the kitchen. "Food first. Then discussion, okay?"

Logan took hold of Cassandra's hand. "You can get your laundry started while Dakota and I get the soup, bread and cheese out. Sound good?"

Cassandra glanced at Dakota and Logan. Dakota winked and nodded. Logan blew her a kiss and squeezed her hand. Words—the things they could convey, say or left unsaid. Maybe Dakota was right. Focusing on something else might dissipate their individual simmering angst. "Sounds good to me. Let me get a load started."

Logan followed Cassandra into the kitchen. He waited until she was in the laundry room before he spoke. "How do you defuse uneasiness?"

"By talking about it." Dakota laid his hand on Logan's shoulder. "We've each got a dynamite word. You also focus on the here and now. Don't let fear lead."

"Sounds like the pep talk you give teen shifters their first full moon change." Logan opened the fridge and took out the bread and cheese. "Working through something with people you trust helps a bunch."

"Exactly. You and I trust each other on many levels. We're in new territory with a shared pair bond courting." Dakota placed the bread and cheese on the table along with the cutting board and a knife.

"We're going to need butter for the bread to pan toast the sandwiches." Cassandra exited the laundry room carrying a plastic bag. "How about toasted ham and cheese sandwiches?"

"With chicken soup?" Dakota leaned against the counter. "Sounds good. Got no problems mixing chicken and pork."

"Me either." Logan rubbed his hands together. "Carnivore first. Omnivorous most of the time."

Dakota laughed as he took the skillet out of the dish drainer. "Most shapeshifters are."

Cassandra moved around the table, putting space between Dakota, Logan and her. "Are you saying you're shapeshifters?'

Dakota turned on a burner and put the skillet on it. "What if Logan and I are? Does that make a difference?"

Cassandra sat in the chair closest to her. "I'm-I'm not sure."

Logan started buttering bread and laying the pieces on the cutting board. "What do you know about shapeshifters?"

Cassandra swiped her sweaty palms on her jeans. "Most are covert. Gossip that the newspaper tries to back up with support. I've read the few books of the xenobiology on it the library has."

Dakota placed two pieces of buttered bread in the skillet. "Okay. You're best friends with Maggie. You know and accept she's magical and a matchmaking witch."

"I know that a few of my neighbors and some of my colleagues are magical or supernatural. This is Cauldron Falls. Humans and the supernatural mixing with the magics." Cassandra glanced at Logan.

Logan handed Dakota two slices of cheese. He picked up the knife and cut a ham slice in two. "Before we discuss this more, let me ask this. Are you afraid of us or what you all of a sudden don't know?"

"Warm the soup on the stove or in the microwave?" Dakota asked, taking the soup container out of the fridge.

"Microwave is okay when we're ready." Cassandra stood. "I can do that."

"It'll be a bit before the last sandwich is ready." Dakota filled the coffeemaker with water and coffee. "I want to hear your thoughts. What's going through your mind?"

"First, there's things we don't know about each other. Second, I don't know why I am befuddled by the possibility you and Logan could be shapeshifters." Cassandra sighed. "Third, fear is trying to drive. Fourth, my subconscious and my educated brain parts are tossing images and shouting things faster than I can process from either one."

Dakota handed Logan three plates. "Maybe the question is have you seen anyone shift? Seen a shapeshifter when they're morphing?"

"No to both questions." Cassandra set three bowls next to the microwave. "From what I read there are many different shapeshifter species."

"Yup, like plants and animals. Even different races and subraces within humans." Dakota turned off the stove, put a sandwich on each plate and placed the skillet in the sink.

"You feel safe with Logan and I, right?" Dakota put spoons, napkins and mugs on the table.

"To a point yes. Neither of you has given me reason to not feel safe." Cassandra poured soup into each bowl. "But, there's always that doubt that says what if."

"Fear popcorning about." Logan held up a box of tea. "This okay for you?"

Cassandra nodded. "Yes, thanks for getting the decaf out."

She put two bowls in the microwave and set the timer. "The doubts and suspicions could happen with humans. Nothing is a hundred percent."

"I'll pour the coffee in a moment. The tea kettle is heating." Dakota sat down at the table. "What you said is true. It comes back to do you trust Logan and me? Feel safe with us?"

"From what I know...yes. From my experiences with each of you—yes. Intimacy wise—can't say. There's a lot I don't know. A bunch of questions running through my head and words popping up from what I remember from the Xenobiology books." Cassandra handed Logan a soup bowl. "Careful it's hot."

"Got it." Logan took the bowl with both hands. "Sounds like Dakota and I need to tell you about our shapeshifter genes."

"Probably a good idea." Dakota set his soup bowl on the table and reached for Cassandra's. "I promise to leave out all the Xenobiology words I can. I couldn't pronounce most of them. My social psychology bachelor's degree and law enforcement minor didn't teach that jargon."

"I don't speak Xenobiology either." Logan held up his mug. "Law enforcement and social science associate degree is best I got."

"The letters behind the name part of our education lives." Cassandra smiled. "Sounds like I'm about to get what Granddad refers to as practical learning aka the truth is often stranger than fiction or how science attempts to explain things."

CHAPTER TEN

"Your granddad was right. Books try to piece together what folks observe. Some can't see beyond what they perceive as the physical universe." Dakota set Cassandra's soup bowl next to her and stood. "Coffee coming up. Your tea will be ready in a few."

Dakota filled his and Logan's mugs with coffee. He turned the burner off under the tea kettle as it started to whistle. He put two tea bags in Cassandra's mug and filled it with water. He handed Cassandra her mug as he continued speaking. "I know for me getting to know about a person includes who and what they are. The what being their likes, desires, and where they come from."

"You mean like are they a certain nationality? Religious views?" Logan sipped his coffee and set the mug down. "Or genetics?"

Dakota picked up his coffee mug, swallowed some and set the mug down. "That could be part of it if the person identifies themselves that way. Who for me is their personal construct. The way they see themselves from the inside out. The what is how the outside world sees them. Reputation. Introvert. Extrovert. The way others describe their construct of the person."

Cassandra sweetened her tea and stirred it. "I'm going to start with how I see me. I'm a librarian. Love reading since I was in elementary school. First job was in a used bookstore. Handling those books let me touch bits and pieces of history lived, read and imagined."

Dakota nodded. He picked up his bowl of soup, slurped some and set the bowl on the table. "Some would say that I ain't got manners for what I did. I like my soup lukewarm. I relish eating good food. I took a few cooking classes in college. I learned to cook for survival. Some people would call me hickish. Yet, I've dined in several world-class restaurants during my summer college travels."

Cassandra nodded. "Thank you both for easing my fears."

Logan held up his sandwich. "Some would call this a grilled ham and cheese. Others toasted ham and cheese. A few a hot ham and cheese sandwich. Perception is personal and universal at the same time."

"Very true." Dakota picked up his sandwich. "I like my sandwich warm and in my stomach. Let's eat."

"I'm with you on that one." Logan bit into his sandwich and chewed. Dakota glanced at Cassandra.

"Food and good company make eating enjoyable." Cassandra tore her sandwich in half and dunked the half in the soup.

They ate in companionable silence until Dulce entered the kitchen. She went to a cabinet close to the back door, pawed at it, and turned, barking. Cassandra pushed back from the table. "All right, Dulce. You're getting a treat. You eat too many and you're going to need to go out again."

Dulce ran out of the kitchen, barking and yipping.

Logan set his empty mug down. "They say animals don't understand what we say."

Dakota laughed. "Dulce understands out and treat. She probably was cussing and fussing with that barking and yipping."

"She probably was." Cassandra set the treat jar on the counter and took two treats out. "She knows she'll go out again before dark after she eats."

Dakota placed his dishes in the sink. "Can we continue our discussion as Logan and I fold our laundry?"

"Let me put my load in the dryer after I get your other dried load out of the dryer." Cassandra handed Dakota her and Logan's dishes. "I've got one more load to do."

"I'll help you with my and Logan's dried load." Dakota set the dishes in the sink.

Logan wheeled toward the living room. "While you and Dakota get the laundry stuff, I'm going to make a few laps around the dining room table on my crutches."

"You sure that's a good idea?" Dakota reached for Logan's crutches.

"Yes. Chairs are close by and I need to get blood circulating in my ass cheeks. Numb butt is no fun." Logan grinned, taking the crutches from Dakota.

Logan balanced the crutch tips on a foot pad of the wheelchair and looped his arm through the open sections. He backed up in short jerky moves. He got close to Dakota and stopped. "Think you could help a buddy get going in the right direction?"

Dakota chuckled. "Depends on which direction. Outside. Hell no! Too damn cold right now. Into the dining room, sure."

Logan snickered. "Sure as hell not going out. Damn wind is too grabby. Dining room please."

"Don't knock yourself out with the crutches." Dakota pushed the wheelchair to the edge of the kitchen doorway and tipped the chair slightly back. "Or me either."

Once Logan and the chair were over the doorway lip into the dining room, Daktoa let go. "Good luck and no crutch speeding. Be back with the laundry in a few."

Dakota paused at the laundry room door. A delicious view greeted him. Cassandra bent over, her luscious ass and hips in full view. He flexed his hands. Grabbing without permission wasn't permitted. Oogling was. He swallowed, blinked and forced his thoughts away from the image forming in his mind. One that his fantasies had summoned more than once. He stepped back and spoke. "Hey Cassandra, what can I help you with?"

"What?" Cassandra straightened. "Oh, it's you, Dakota. You startled me. Lost in my thoughts."

"Care to share 'em?" Dakota entered the laundry room. "Logan is crutching around the dining room getting some exercise."

Cassandra smiled, handing him the laundry basket. "He's used to being on his feet active. I bet he's antsy sitting so much."

"Neither of us spends much time sitting some days." Dakota took the basket. "You okay? Anything you want to share?"

Cassandra hastily grabbed her laundry out to the hamper, tossing it into the washer. "Self-talk. Something I do when my thoughts are jumbled. Nothing special."

Dakota set the basket on the dryer. He faced Cassandra, his arms spread. "Hug? Touch is important. Seeing you skittish is not something I want happening."

Cassandra pressed her lips together. Dakota asked for a hug. Not some half-morphed human animal. She'd seen him and Logan bare-assed naked. Spent the night safely with them under the same roof. Why should now be any different? After this morning's view, she wanted to touch and hug. Her libido kept nudging her with urges. Urges to touch, kiss, hug and—do more. Cassandra blinked, stepping forward. "Hugs are good."

She moved tighter to Dakota until the tips of their slippers touched. She leaned forward, wrapping her arms loosely around Dakota's waist. Her forehead rested against his chest.

"Mind if I hug you tightly?" Dakota laid his arms light on her shoulders. "Quick, tight embrace and let go. I learned in psychology that fast hugs sometimes are better for breaking the ice."

Cassandra tipped her head back. "There's no ice just wanting to not invade space. I've read some shapeshifters didn't like tight quarters."

Dakota hugged her tightly, brushed his lips over hers and let go. "There are a few that don't. Logan and I aren't one of those."

"We better check on Logan," Cassandra said, stepping back. She closed the washer lid and pushed the start button. "Thank you for the hug."

Dakota picked up the laundry basket. "You bet. I saw some maple walnut ice cream in the freezer. That with some hot fudge sauce makes a fine dessert."

"You still hungry?" Cassandra moved past Dakota.

"Depends on what kind of hunger you're talking about." Dakota winked and entered the dining room.

Cassandra slowly exhaled. Dakota didn't wear aftershave. Yet, his scent lingered around her as if he marked her. The same thing had happened with Logan at two Sadie Hawkins dances. Same with Dakota. Logan's distinct scent had rushed over her as she and talked earlier. Had Dakota and Logan remarked and reclaimed like she read about?

"Okay speedy. Time for a break," Dakota called out, entering the dining room.

"No breaks needed." Logan sat in a chair at the end of the dining room table. "Sprain is bad enough. Stop cursing me."

Dakota chuckled. "Words can be deceiving for sure. Good thing neither of us are magics."

"One of the reasons basic magic is a required course throughout high school and university. Knowing the caution words damn well helps." Logan put both hands on the table and tried to stand.

"I think the caution word here is overdoing." Dakota reached for the crutch closest to him.

"I'm ready for something sweet." Logan winked, adding, "Kissing Cassandra can wait till later."

"I figured you weren't referring to me." Dakota laughed and shook his head. "Besides the maple walnut ice, there's cookie dough in the fridge."

"Fresh baked cookies and ice cream." Logan rubbed his stomach. "Yum."

"I hate to interrupt such synctilating conversation." Cassandra pulled the closest basket of laundry to her. "Folding first. Cookies and ice cream second."

"I'll get the wheelchair." Dakota leaned the crutches against the table. "Logan, help Cassandra sort what's yours from mine."

Logan dropped back into the chair he'd been sitting in. He glanced at Cassandra. "Sure you're ready to fold our briefs and stuff?"

Cassandra turned the basket over on the table. "Not like I don't know what men's underwear looks like. I've seen you both naked."

Logan ducked his head. When had the room's temperature changed? Damn, it got hot in there suddenly.

Cassandra set the basket upright. She walked over to Logan, leaned down and kissed his cheek. "Nice to know you still can blush."

"I'm not." Logan looked up.

"Dude, why are your cheeks flushed?" Dakota pushed the wheelchair into the dining room, stopping next to Logan.

"Caught him off guard." Cassandra dumped the second basket on the table. "Thinks folding your clothes is going to embarrass me."

"You're doing your own laundry." Dakota placed the second basket on the floor close to the table.

Logan moved into the wheelchair. "How about we change the subject?"

Cassandra picked up a pair of purple-colored briefs. "Sure. Who these belong to?"

Logan grabbed the briefs. "Tossing a mixed load in the washer is easier when you don't have to worry about colors bleeding."

Cassandra held up another pair of briefs. Common men cut briefs sold in most department stores and online. "Must be Dakota's."

"What if they are?" Dakota snagged the briefs out of Cassandra's hand. "We haven't seen your underwear yet?"

Logan coughed. "How did we get started on this?"

Dakota tossed the briefs at Logan. "Question and comments made."

Cassandra placed a folded shirt in the basket next to her. "You're both interested in me. I know bits and pieces about you. Same with you about me. Each of you tell me something about you I don't know."

Dakota sorted socks out of the pile and began pairing them up. "Okay. I'm part of the Grey Wolf clan out of Montana. We can shift at will. Don't need a full moon to get furry. My great-grandsire was the last direct lineage alpha. We vote for our leaders."

Cassandra handed him three pairs of socks. "When do you get furry?"

Dakota looked up. Cassandra's gaze met his without looking away. "Family reunions. Weddings, pair bondings, and when I feel like it. Usually in warmer weather for sure. No need to get frostbite on vital parts."

Cassandra smirked. "Neither of you need that."

"Logan and I can sort out who's is who's later." Dakota smiled, tossing the paired socks into the basket next to the t-shirts Cassandra folded. "Logan, your turn to share something Cassandra doesn't know."

"Common things Dakota and I share are we shift when we want. Getting furry isn't a priority for us. We're part of the oddballs according to our pack clans." Logan pushed the basket closer to the one between Cassandra and Dakota. He placed two stacks of folded briefs in the basket. "Brindle Wolf pack is a small clan from northwestern Texas panhandle. In case you're wondering, I can't shift and heal. Isn't part of my genetic makeup."

Cassandra stood. "Thanks for sharing your secrets with me."

Logan took her hand. "Not secrets. Facts of who we are. You okay with that?"

Dakota took her other hand. "Is fear still threatening to swamp you?"

Cassandra shook her head and squeezed Dakota and Logan's hands. "Not scared. Processing probably the best word. Layering it with what I already know about you."

"Then I've got a question for you." Dakota let go of her hand. "Logan asked you earlier about a triad. How do you feel about Logan and I courting you?"

CHAPTER ELEVEN

"Both of you?" Cassandra faced Logan and turned back to Dakota. "At the same time? Competing against each other? Me?"

"You, yes. No competition." Logan picked up the basket and set it on his lap. "At the same time with mutual consent from each other."

"Is that acceptable?" Cassandra reached for the last folded clothes. Maggie and her matchmaker friends talked about the different family and pair-bonding configurations among the supernaturals and magics.

Dakota picked up the last of his and Logan's folded clothes. "Acceptable. Done and sometimes encouraged."

"I'm not one of you." Cassandra stepped away from the table. The dryer's buzzer sounded. "Interspecies mating is accepted and allowed by treaty. I don't remember that including humans. Mere mortals as I've heard a few refer to humans."

"Here's the thing," Dakota began, moving toward the stairs. "There's intermingling of supernaturals, magics and humans."

Logan wheeled toward the steps, following Dakota. "Some humans and supernaturals are pair-bonded monogamously. Some are same-sex. Others, male and female. Then there's quads, group marriages, and what Dakota and I are hoping to form with you. A triad."

"Cassandra, can you bring the other basket up?." Dakota started up the steps. "Logan, Cassandra and I will be down in a couple moments. See if you can get Dulce's coat on her. She keeps going over to the back door."

Cassandra picked up the basket Logan held out and followed Dakota up the stairs. At the top of the steps, Dakota paused. "I'd like to talk in private for a few moments."

Cassandra glanced back down the stairs. Logan waved and wheeled off toward the kitchen calling Dulce's name. She gripped the basket tighter. Was this the first I'm the best speeches? Deities help her if she had to choose between either Dakota or Logan. She didn't want to lose their friendship or break theirs up.

"Sure." She stepped onto the upper landing and moved around Dakota. "We can sort yours and Logan's things while we talk."

Dakota nodded. "Humans and magics have pair-bonded too. Some are in Sadie Hawkins's full moon matches."

"Sadie Hawkins?" Cassandra sat on the bed, setting the basket next to her.

Dakota put his basket on the bed and sat cross-legged on the floor. "You've met Siobhan, the owner of Sadie's."

"Yes. You, Logan and I have attended a couple of their events. Full moon happenings on one or two I remember." Cassandra dumped one basket on the bed. She set the empty basket on the floor between her and Dakota.

"Those briefs and t-shirts are mine." Dakota pointed to the stacks closest to her. "The matchmaker's council plus the magics and supernaturals councils passed an edict three decades back that if the third Saturday of the month had a full moon, those were Sadie Hawkins times. Women got first choice for mates."

"Kinda leveling the playing field, I see." Cassandra handed Dakota the briefs and t-shirts. "What's that got to do with our discussion?"

"This weekend is a full moon and blue moon weekend. Back-to-back full moons. Double Sadie Hawkins." Dakota stood up. "You can two men if you want. Logan and I are voicing our interest."

A few moments passed as Dakota and Cassandra finished sorting clothes into the baskets.

"I'd like to spend a night with you. Holding you and cuddling." Dakota held out his hand. "Logan would too. You and me one night. You and Logan another."

Cassandra slowly inhaled. If she said yes, did that include sex? Was that expected? Expectations and consent blurred. She needed clarity.

"Let me think about this." Cassandra picked up the basket containing Logan's clothes. "Take this into Logan's room, please. I'll meet you downstairs momentarily."

Cassandra walked into her room and closed the door. She dropped into the wingback chair in her reading corner. What had she gotten herself into?

Two hunks who desire you. Two men who accept you. Two...

"Enough psyche! I can count." Cassandra gripped the arms of the chair, ready to jump up and pace.

What's pacing going to get done? You spend more time watching where you're walking to not stub your toes than thinking. How about pen and paper? Q and A time?

She stood, walked over to the dresser, and opened her work tote bag. Inside were her workbadge, key ring clipped to the badge lanyard, and the two note pads she carried plus a few pens. One pad contained meeting notes and possible new book additions to the library. The other pad was her thought jot pad. Recipes, musings and a

few stick people sketches. She grinned as she leafed through the pad. Wasn't her diary. Nor would it become that. What she wrote no one would see. Once she was done, shred and shred again would happen.

She tapped the pad with the pen wondering what her top questions were. Both Dakota and Logan were prime catches in her mind. Gentle, caring and unafraid of showing it with her. Not that either was into PDAs much. A kiss on the cheek or maybe a brief hug. Neither of them ranked over the other. Both caught her attention. Certainly ignited her desire, given her fantasies and earlier reactions to seeing them naked. Both were here because she trusted them. Her grandparents vouched for each of them, provided references and even campaigned for their re-elections. Dakota and Logan kept Sylvan Valley and Cauldron Falls safe. Could she let them into her inner sanctum? Let her guard down and trust them implicitly? Trust them with her heart?

Who did she spend the night with first? Her bed wasn't big enough for all three.

Cassandra shivered. Some women hinted and smiled when three and one bed topics came up at the Sadie Hawkins events as they mingled and ate. Three in one bed—not her thing. One-on-one suited her just fine. Everyone had their preferences and one at a time in bed was hers. She and Dulce liked to sprawl. Room for one more okay. Room for two there wasn't. A queen-sized bed had only so much room.

Would Dakota mind his feet hanging off the end? Mind Dulce snuggling between them from time to time? Logan would need to be closer to the bathroom. Easier access for him. Would he mind sleeping with her after Dakota had? What were Dakota's preferences?

She stood, tossed the pen and pad on her bed and exited the bedroom. Too many questions without answers. Answers that needed input from the two gents awaiting her downstairs. There were a few hours until one of them entered her and Dulce's inner sanctum.

Dakota set the basket with Logan's clothes on the bed. Logan's clothes from last night were tossed on the foot of the bed. Dakota smiled and turned. They were enough alike that some things didn't bother either of them like stripping and dropping into bed after a twelve-hour shift. Straightening up came when they got up or on cleaning day. In other ways, they were very different individuals. Logan preferred cotton thermals and wool hunting socks as part of his winter wear. Dakota shuddered. Get wool near him and he broke out in hives. Allergic and calamine lotion were two things he steered clear of as much as possible.

As he entered the hall, Dakota glanced toward Cassandra's room. The door opened. Cassandra nodded, flashed him a weak grin and started down the stairs. Was something bothering her? The only way he was going to find out was follow her downstairs.

Logan moved to the couch, laying Dulce's coat next to him. The scamp ducked under the table twice, stayed out of reach and growled when he grabbed her collar. Let her think she bluffed her way out of putting her coat on. "Okay, Dulce, you win. You don't have to put on your coat. It's gonna be pretty cold when you go out."

Dulce squirmed her way up on the couch as he laid his hand palm up with a treat on it.

"You want the treat?" Logan opened and closed his hand around the treat.

Dulce barked and whined.

"No coat. No treat." Logan opened and closed his hand twice. He held up Dulce's coat with his other hand. "Put the coat on and you get the treat. Maybe two treats."

Dulce barked, nuzzled his fist and backed up. She crept forward a few steps, jumping back as he opened his hand. "You want the treat; coat first."

Dulce barked twice. She turned away and sat with her back to him.

Logan pressed his lips together, trying hard to not snort and smirk. Impish pug! A lot better than a piss ant chihuahua named Chuy.

"I guess you don't want this." Logan turned, hiding the coat between his legs, as he laid the treat on the cushion between him and Dulce. He laid his arm on the back of the couch.

Dulce lunged toward the treat. Logan leaned forward, arm raised and—GOAL!

Dulce growled, barked, and squirmed more.

"You get your treat in a moment." Logan pulled Dulce's coat from between his legs.

"I'll help you with that." Cassandra snagged the coat out of his hand. "Dulce, sit. *Now.*"

Dulce stopped squirming, yipped, and lunged toward Logan.

Logan reached for Ducle with his other hand. Flesh, warm and soft, slid over the back of his hand and came into sight as Cassandra gripped Ducle's collar next to where he held on.

Cassandra dropped onto the couch. "Take hold before I let go."

Logan nodded and wrapped his hand around part of Ducle's collar. "Got her."

Dakota came into view as Logan tipped his head back. "Like wrestling a toddler to get em dressed or buck assed naked for a bath."

Cassandra snickered. Logan snorted. Dakota muttered and held his hand out. "I'll handle the coat. You hold her fast."

Dulce ducked her head to the left. Dakota copied Dulce's movements. Barks and growls sounded. The coat slipped over Dulce's head. Muffled barks and yips followed. More squirming.

Dakota stepped back. "Coat started. Now the rest is up to you and Logan."

"Thank you." Cassandra quickly eased the rest of the coat over Dulce's front legs and paws.

Logan dropped two treats on the couch in front of Dulce. "You behaved some. You earned your treats."

Dulce grabbed the treats, jumped off the couch and ran toward the kitchen. Cassandra walked toward the kitchen. "She thinks she's sly. In a few moments, she is going to try running past me."

"I'll go out with her. I need to check on the driveway." Dakota followed Cassandra into the kitchen.

Dakota leaned against the counter, watching Cassandra looking out the backdoor windows. She glanced at him and went back to looking out the window. Was she avoiding him?

"Is something wrong?" He picked up his hikers and sat in the chair closest to him. He quickly tied the laces and stood. "Did I say something wrong?"

"No," Cassandra faced him. "Dulce ran into the laundry room. She thinks she's fooled me."

"Want me to get her?" Dakota started toward the laundry room.

"Let her be for a moment." Cassandra closed the space between them. "You asked me something upstairs."

"I asked a couple of things." Dakota shoved his hands into his jeans pockets. Putting them on Cassandra's shoulders probably wasn't a good idea.

"Your hug was great. Thanks." Cassandra held a finger to her lip. "Dulce is trying to sneak out. The answer to your second question is cuddling with you or Logan all night sounds great. We need to talk more about that."

Dakota kissed Cassandra's cheek, spun around and leaned down. He scooped Dulce up midspurt past him. He held her eye level with him. "Scamp, you can't outdo a wolfish shapeshifter. I'm going out with you."

Moments later, Dakota and Dulce exited the kitchen. Cassandra touched her lips and cheek. He'd hugged her, kissed her cheek again and her lips twice while holding Dulce. He handed Dulce to her long enough to get his coat and watch cap on. Saluted her, took Dulce from her and walked outside. Cold air had rushed over her the moment Dakota opened the door. Why was she ready to fan herself? Images of him nude and prepared to claim her flashed through her mind.

Logan wheeled into the kitchen. His ankle throbbed and pinged worse than it had all day. "Cassandra, where are my pain. . ." He stopped speaking. Cassandra faced the back door like she was staring at something. Was something wrong?

He wheeled closer and touched Cassandra's hand. "Are you okay?"

Cassandra looked down at him, nodding. "I think so."

"You wanna talk about it?" Logan squeezed Cassandra's hand and let go.

CHAPTER TWELVE

"When Dakota gets back in, yes." Cassandra opened the cabinet closest to her. "You said something about pain. Aspirin or something stronger?"

"Aspirin and an ice pack for now. Doctor said use the prescription he gave me at night mostly." Logan propped his ankle up on the chair closest to him. "I probably overdid it crutching around as much as I did. It felt good in the moment."

Cassandra handed Logan a glass of water and set the open bottle of aspirin on the table. "Yeah, a few friends from the leather community say pain is so close to pleasure. Not for me."

Logan saluted her with the glass and popped two aspirins in his mouth. She filled a gallon plastic storage bag with ice from the freezer. "Homemade ice pack coming up. Keep it wrapped in the towel."

"Yep. Ten minutes on. Five minutes off. Flex ankle and knee some. Ice pack back on for five to seven more minutes. Dull the pain down to manageable." Logan took the towel-wrapped ice-filled bag from her. He placed it on his ankle and yawned. "After we talk, I'm going down for a nap."

Cassandra put the aspirin away and the glass in the sink. "There's a chaise lounger in your room plus a recliner. We can comfortably sit and talk while you lay on the bed."

Logan gave her two thumbs up as the backdoor opened.

"Come on scamp. I'm not chasing you and Chuy around your dog yard again. Mrs. Abernathy and I are not dodging ice for your enjoyment." Dakota quickly closed the door and held Dulce out to Cassandra.

"Chuy got out?" Cassandra set Dulce on the counter and started removing her coat. "Is Mrs. Abernathy all right?"

"Yeah. Chuy shot past her when she came out on the porch as I swept snow off her steps.' Dakota hung his coat and watch cap on the coat pegs. "He followed Dulce into her dog yard. Took his turn leaving evidence of his visit. He's back inside with Mrs. Abernathy."

"Chuy's living up to his neighborhood reputation." Cassandra laid Dulce's coat on the counter. "Friends with everybody. He and Dulce are best buds."

"I overheard Mrs. Abernathy scolding him as I finished clearing her steps." Dakota grinned as he set Dulce on the floor. "Told his fixed. His Romeo days are long gone."

"Now that the neighborhood ambassador is safe behind closed doors, I'm ready for round two." Logan held up the wrapped ice pack. "I need to stretch out."

"I'm changing the subject." Cassandra put the ice pack in the sink. Logan and Dakota's gaze met hers. "We've skirted around something. Something I think we need to talk about."

"Are you sure you're ready?" Dakota slipped his feet into his slippers.

"Logan and I figured out the best place to do this was in his room. Chaise lounge and recliner are available to relax in. He can stretch out on the bed and prop his ankle up."

Dakota faced Logan. "You ready to for this?"

Logan nodded. With your help, I can get up the steps. Talking and getting a conversation started that might be in bits and pieces."

"All right." Dakota faced Cassandra. "One digression first. Is your laundry done?"

"Everything is in the hamper, ready to take upstairs and fold later."

"I'll take the hamper up. Be back down to help Logan up the stairs in a moment." Dakota quickly brushed past Cassandra.

Logan held out his hand. "Think we caught him off guard."

"Possibly. We've all done that at some point today." Cassandra clasped Logan's hand and let go.

Dakota passed them carrying the hamper. "Caught off guard is what we all are right now. I think we're at a point where discussion is what we've got to do."

Logan wheeled after Dakota. Cassandra shrugged and followed Dakota and Logan out of the kitchen. Dulce following her.

Dakota set the hamper on the first step and turned. "I'm not angry. Confused and unsure aren't familiar things for me. I am usually the one initiating and doing the courting one-on-one. Hadn't teamed up with someone in a while. Nor really discussed this with Logan until on our way over here."

Logan stopped close to the stairs. "Sorry if I overstepped boundaries."

Dakota smiled. "No boundaries in place, dude. We're all friends. None of us anticipated being here and discussing this now."

Cassandra reached for the hamper. "Nor did I anticipate folding your unmentionables. Or you lugging my clothes up and down the stairs."

"All part of the plan?" Dakota chuckled. "Seriously, I think we've all stepped into new territory. We're unsure how to go about this."

"That's for sure." Cassandra tugged the hamper to her. "I can get this up the steps."

Dakota pulled the hamper away from her. "I'm going say something that needs said. We're in this together. Not anyone of us alone. Logan and I want and are going to help as we can. That doesn't mean you are helpless nor are we. We work as a team. It takes all of us to survive. And beyond now we'll work more things out, I am sure."

Cassandra glanced at Logan. He nodded and added, "What he said, and I'll add this. We've each got our personal boundaries. We'll learn about each other and ourselves as we talk."

Cassandra sighed. "Okay. We don't have to worry about introducing the kid," she pointed to Dulce "and worrying about how she's going to accept things."

Logan burst out laughing. "Except when her boyfriend Chuy comes around."

"Yeah, he growled at me when I stepped between them." Dakota grinned. "Looks like there's a bunch of courting going on in the neighborhood."

Dulce barked, turning around in circles when she heard Chuy's name.

Cassandra shook her head, sighed again and shrugged. "How about we call it getting to know each other for the moment and go from there? Courting sounds too formal for me right now."

"Go at a pace we're all comfortable with sounds like the best option." Logan wheeled to the dining room table and grabbed his crutches. "Dakota, let's get me upstairs first since I am the largest moving obstacle."

Dakota let go of the hamper. "Both of us are large moving obstacles as we go up the stairs. How about Cassandra and the hamper go first? If she needs to call for help, she is in the clear."

"Yeah, maybe Chuy can redeem himself by running down the street barking and getting someone to rally to his battle cry. Hopefully not Mrs. Abernathy!" Logan chuckled. "Just trying to figure how to get me prone easily so my blasted ankle stops throbbing and I can nap."

"Not the first time she's gone upstairs this way." Cassandra scooped up Dulce, opened the hamper and set her inside. Cassandra hefted the hamper up three steps and glanced over her shoulder. Logan and Dakota stood at the bottom of the stairs staring up at her while Logan stuffed one crutch under each arm. "I suggest you grab the banister and lean on Dakota so you and the crutches don't win another wrestling match."

Logan shot her a thumbs up. He held up one crutch. "Good idea. These things got a mind of their own."

Dakota chortled. "My Mam used to say all things are alive. Watch how you talk to them. They might bite back."

Cassandra tipped the hamper down as she reached the top stair. Dulce jumped out, shook and raced into the bedroom. Cassandra moved the hamper closer to her bedroom door. She turned back ready to assist Dakota and Logan as needed. One step up followed by a slight hop and muttered curse continued for the next few moments.

Logan reached out to her as he and Dakota reached the top step. Cassandra clasped Logan's hand and steadied him. "Using your left hand to grip when you a righty ain't easy."

"In reverse for me. Lefty using right to balance." Dakota placed one crutch under Logan's arm. "Was easier that way than what we tried this morning."

"Yeah. I thought about sitting on my ass and sliding down the steps. Hard part would have been getting seated and then how the hell did I stand back up." Logan put the second crutch under his other arm. "Praise the powers that be this is just a bad sprain."

"Safer too than trying to walk the stairs backwards and heft you and the wheelchair up at same time." Dakota moved past Logan. "Let's get you situated. That way we can all chillax and shift gears."

"Not moving from here for a bit." Logan dropped onto the bed. He tossed two pillows toward the foot of the bed. "Gotta prop the ankle up."

Dakota fluffed the pillows. "One under the other?"

"Start with one for now." Logan stuffed the two others behind him. "Thanks both of you. Appreciate the help."

Cassandra leaned down and kissed his cheek. "We need each other to do more than survive."

Dakota dropped into the recliner and groaned. "Muscles sighing out loud."

Cassandra sat on the chaise lounge opposite side of the room. "Thank you for checking on my neighbors and Mrs. Abernathy. You've done a lot."

"All part of taking care of the community. Your granddad asked me about how important community is to me. He asked Logan the same thing before referring him to Sylvan Valley Chief of Police." Dakota slumped down in the recliner. "What's the first question you've got?"

Cassandra gripped the sides of the chaise as she uprighted herself. She swung her feet over the side and sat up. "How long have you known I was the one?"

"Depends on what you mean by the one?" Logan asked.

"The person you wanted to date, see, or even focus on most?"

"I've known for a while. Problem was coordinating time to talk. My job was nonstop for a while until the city council gave me a budget to hire. Deputy help and the college security staff enlarging helped too." Dakota pointed to Logan. "What about you, Logan?"

"Scent. Your pheromones reached up and slam-dunked me two Sadie Hawkins ago. Your aura flashed mauve and blue for me. I know that other colors show up for some people and matchmakers go by certain colors for matching folks." Logan flashed a quick grin. "Deployment and classes plus work—you know the drift."

Cassandra nodded. "Between recent elections, changes in the university management chain and keeping up on job duties, I so get where you are coming from."

Dakota stretched and yawned. "My wolf picked up your scent after our second dance at the first Sadie Hawkins event we met at. Aura reading isn't one of my strong abilities."

"Non magical I learned to trust my gut. Sounds like Granddad was doing some matchmaking on his own with the community question. He's big on making sure Cauldron Falls citizens feel safe and accurately represented."

"He mentioned you a couple of times," Logan offered. "I figured he was using you as a frame of reference. Someone I could touch base with and ask questions. Didn't know he was referring me to Sylvan Valley Police."

"Granddad stepped out of politics after he got elected mayor for the third time. Grandma told him there was more to life than running around town checking up on everyone. The university started during his last term. He served on the board for three years until the travel bug bit and grandma declared retirement was for traveling."

"Sounds like we've cleared the air some with that question. My question is are you interested in more than friendship?"

Cassandra swallowed twice, pressed her lips together and considered her response. She was interested. Both intrigued her. Twice over. Both at the same time? That is something she hadn't considered. Concept wasn't wholly new to her. Some of Maggie's friends were in multiperson relationships and families. Monogamous worked for some. Others chose their family structure according to their choices.

"Yes, I am interested. But . . ." How did she express her hesitation? Where did it come from? New territory? She hadn't given much thought to multiperson relationships. Understanding xenobiology and new class research books plus promotion to head librarian had grabbed her focus for several weeks and the last few months. "I hesitate because I haven't given dating much thought. Two at the same time is new for me, too."

"How about a checklist? Agreed upon topics or questions and we approach them as they come up?" Dakota sat up. "We need pen and paper to do that."

Logan yawned again. "I'm not keeping up with things. Too sleepy."

"Brings up the topic of sleep and bedmates. Doesn't mean more than what any of us agree to. Like Logan and I are not sexually interested in each other."

Cassandra slowly sat on the bed. "A necessary topic, *right now*?"

"Had to come up at some point." Dakota stretched and stood. "Things could change as things progress. Nothing is set in stone."

"Change is part of the ongoing conversation. We're learning from each other as we interact." Logan raised his leg some, wiggled and slid down on the bed further. "Right now, cuddles are as far as I go and a blanket to do it under."

"Chose your cuddler. Dulce or . . ." Dakota picked up the quilt off the foot of the bed and tossed it over Logan.

"How about Cassandra?" Logan grimaced as he rolled on his side. "Nothing more than warm cuddles and a good nap."

"Safe space is negotiable and honored." Dakota brushed his lips over Cassandra's. "You decide what works for you. I'm going to my room."

Logan held up the quilt. "Please stay. Cuddles nothing more."

Cassandra kicked off her shoes and reached for the quilt. "Cuddles welcomed."

Logan pulled a pillow from behind his head, plumped it and laid it next to him. Cassandra stretched out beside Logan, pulling the quilt over both of them. "No sex now. Nap. Talk more later."

Logan rolled closer to her, laid his hand on her waist and murmured, "All good."

Logan's breath warmed her neck as sleep claimed him. Cassandra blinked and pulled the quilt over her shoulders. Dulce jumped up on the bed and settled next to her.

CHAPTER THIRTEEN

Dakota flopped on his bed. His bloody control nerd wolf could stop howling and growling. Territorial he wasn't. Or was he? He share-dated before. Dealt with his. . . How the hell could he be jealous?

Cuz she's the one. The mate you're looking for. Full moon match that you and your heart acknowledged. Possession is part of the marking. You will know who your partner is. Accept and enjoy.

How the hell did he integrate all this? Processing was a bitch. A needed one. He pressed all his fingertips against the mattress. One, Logan was his best friend. They'd talked about mutual interest before. Not to this point. Their first "our lady" happened on their way over. Lots of stuff happening all at once.

What are you going to do about this? Talking about it in front of Cassandra? Include Cassandra in the discussion?

Dakota pressed both ring fingers against the mattress. Two things to consider. How many more? Could any of them be resolved quickly? Easily?

He inhaled slowly, pressing his index and middle fingertips on the mattress. Next item was a combination of what does Cassandra wants, Logan wants and his wants. Needs tinged things as well. Definitions and explanations mixed with what-ifs and what about plans.

Dude, you need to write things down. Prioritize them. What you want and need. Your understanding and what questions you have. Don't expect expectations to be met on the first try. Like negotiating yearly work contracts.

Dakota flexed his hands, turned on his side and drew his knees to his chest. His eyes closed as he slowly inhaled. He held his breath to a four-count and exhaled to a similar count. He repeated the cycle three more times until his psyche opened. His wolf rushed forward, tail wagging and yipping. They circled each other thrice. His wolf moved back and sat on his haunches. Dakota sat cross-legged, his hands extended palms up in front of him.

Greetings my wolf. I seek wisdom and insight. My mate is found. Another claims her too. Is this the circle of three you counseled me on?

Greetings my human. Three hearts entwined is the symbol you seek. Each of you knows what you seek. Allow the hearts to speak. Hear each other out. Questions will come and answers will follow. Allow your heart and psyche to guide you.

His wolf nuzzled and licked his hands, turned and bolted back into the cloud he appeared from. Yips and barks echoed back. The last howl echoed a lingering message. *Trust each other. You will each lead. Trust and ask your hearts to speak.*

Dakota stretched out, relaxing his arms and legs. His sleep mantra filled his thoughts. Sleep deep. Rest and restore. His breathing slowed as his subconscious flashed images of his heart's desire.

Logan slowly opened his eyes. The sun cast shadows dancing across the wall indicated evening was nigh. Sunset colors swelled over the ice and frost crystals coating the windowpanes.

Cassandra stirred next to him. She'd cuddled closer as they slept. He'd managed to get to get to the bathroom and back without battling the crutches. Mutual cooperation was great. Sitting on the commode giggling prompted belly laughs he'd managed to keep his chortles at a low level. Dulce had padded into the bathroom, demanded pets, sat at his feet as if she enjoyed sharing his momentary gaiety and followed him out as far as Dakota's room and entered.

Logan rolled onto his back. Had Cassandra slept? He hoped she had. Relaxing was vital if they were going to hear each other. Actively listening and hearing took focus. Focus on the ongoing conversation meant not reading his interpretation into what Dakota or Cassandra said. Asking questions, paraphrasing and mirror helped.

Cassandra rolled toward him. "Hi," she sleepily murmured. "I didn't realize how tired I was."

"Glad you got some sleep." Logan trailed his fingers across Cassandra's cheek. "How you doing?"

"Better centered. Realized I panicked. Let fear drive in a way I didn't recognize." Cassandra tossed the quilt off her. "Where's Dulce?"

"In with Dakota." Logan sat up and scooted to the edge of the bed. "My ankle's doing better. I'm glad I don't need the stronger meds."

"Three's a group discussion?" Dakota stood close to the edge of the bedroom door. "Not interrupting something, am I?"

"Didn't get an eyeful, did you?" Logan snickered. "No flashing body parts, right?"

"Dang, you mean I missed it?' Dakota perched on the arm of the recliner and shrugged.

Cassandra rolled to the edge of the bed and sat up. "I'm fully dressed. So's Logan. Any flashing wasn't on my part."

"Ice breaker." Dakota swiped his sweaty palms down his jeans. He slowly inhaled and summoned his inner wolf calm. In the corner of his eye, his wolf appeared. "What's next?"

"My turn to ask a question." Cassandra pulled her shoes on. "Does sleeping together have to include sex?"

Logan snorted. "We slept together and no sex happened."

"Right," Cassandra stretched. "I'm not saying sex will or won't happen. I want to know if either of you are expecting it to happen."

"I'm attracted to you." Dakota rested his hands on his knees. "Expecting sex, no. Open to sex happening one on one, yes. Not into group acrobatics."

"Me neither. Group hugs and cuddles are great. Sex is a spectator sport." Logan clasped his leg behind his knee and raised it. "I'm pretty sure Dakota agrees with me on this. Neither of us are voyeurs. Lovers yes. Want our lady to enjoy making love with each of us. There's no competition going on."

Cassandra reached up, touched her lips and lowered her hand. Her mouth wasn't hanging open. Dakota winked when she looked at him and Logan kept stretching each leg. She wet her lips."Are you trying to shock me? Or pluck my nerve?"

"Neither sweetie." Dakota walked over to the bed and sat next to her. "Logan summed it. More explicitly than I did. Each of us has a say in how fast this moves, how it moves and where things go. There's a saying: keep the conversation flowing without overwhelming all involved."

"What if I'm not ready to be sexual with either of you?" Cassandra drew her knees up onto the bed and wrapped her arms tightly around them, hugging herself tightly.

Dakota moved to the end of the bed. "This isn't about jumping bones here and now. Or even putting a hashmark on the calendar as to the exact date and time."

"What he said." Logan rolled on his side. "We're attracted. You're attracted, right?"

Cassandra nodded. "I'm attracted."

"I'll be back in a moment." Dakota stood, walked to the bedroom door and turned back. "Think about what questions you want to ask and in what order. I'll explain more when I get back."

Logan laid his hand on Cassandra's. "Are you okay?"

"On some levels, yes. Others, not sure."Cassandra shrugged. "New things. Unusual things. It's like being on a first date."

Logan smiled. "Playing catch up in a unique way. We're getting to know each other better. In a group setting instead of one on one."

"That's it. Plus knowing openly both of you are interested and attracted to me without being jealous."

"Depends on your definition of jealousy." Dakota entered the bedroom carrying three pens and a pad. "I was a bit jealous of Logan this afternoon. He got to cuddle and sleep with you."

"Sorry, Dakota," Logan began, trying to sit up. "If I had known . ."

"Nothing to be sorry about." Dakota cut Logan off. "I was envious. You were doing something I wanted to do. Not upset you got to do it. My turn will come."

"Are you saying jealousy and envy are two different things?" Cassandra sat in the recliner.

"Yes. Envy is wanting what someone else has. Jealousy is wanting what someone else has and if you can't have it, neither can they. Understanding and owning what you're feeling is not easy sometimes." Dakota tore two pages off the pad and handed them with a pen to Cassandra.

Logan took a pen and two sheets of paper from Dakota. "Don't worry about understanding it all. Every pair bonding and group bonding has their own paths they've worked through. What is your idea Dakota, with the questions?"

Dakota sat on the bed. "Conversation starters based on our questions. Tear the paper in half and write a question on each. Don't number them. Fold them in half and put them on the bed. We mix em up and pick one to ask each of us."

"Sounds good to me." Logan ripped his sheets in two. "On the count of three?"

Cassandra hastily tore her sheets in two. Dakota did the same.

"Go for it." Dakota held his pen up. "Ready Cassandra?"

"I think so." Cassandra balanced her pages on her lap.

"Go." Logan started writing. He folded his first half and tossed it on the bed between them. He glanced at Dakota and Cassandra. Each was writing and folding paper. Logan wrote his next three questions, folded the paper, and put it on top of Cassandra's and Dakota's folded pieces.

"I'll put your pens with mine." Dakota laid the three pens on the nightstand. "Cassandra, do you want to mix up or draw the first question?"

"I could do both." Cassandra scooted back on the bed until she could see Dakota and Logan at the same time.

"One or the other." Dakota grinned and winked. "Logan said go. You or I mix. The person who doesn't mix draws the first question."

"I'll mix." Cassandra picked up the paper pieces with both hands and laid them down. She mixed up left to right, right to left. "Okay. Mixing done."

"This question is for all three of us. No matter who's question it is." Dakota plucked the top piece on the pile. He unfolded the slip and read. "Why hadn't we declared our interest before now?"

"Cassandra, can you put this under my ankle?" Logan held one of his pillows out. I'll answer first. I was away. For me declaring interest is something done face to face."

Dakota nodded. "Agreed. I knew I was interested. Wasn't sure how to approach the subject. How do you tell one of your closest friends hey I'm interested in more?"

Cassandra lifted Logan's ankle and placed the pillow under it as she answered. "My answer is pretty much the same. Work, friendship and time to let the others involved know. I value our friendships. The connection we have with each other is special and amazing."

Dakota placed the paper on the nightstand. "I'm going to ask my fifth question. Are we ready to trust our friendship and connection to move to another level?"

"We must or we wouldn't be here talking like this." Cassandra picked up a slip. "After Logan answers, I'm reading the next written question."

"Trust is earned. We've known each other for a couple of years now. I'm ready to move to the next level. Relationship discussions."

Cassandra glanced down at the open sheet she held. She sighed and rolled her eyes. "I think the powers that be are signaling us. Next question is what is our relationship diagram?"

Dakota chuckled. "I'll own up to that one. Elda, one of Cauldron Falls' premiere matchmakers, talked about group dynamics at one of the recent Sadie Hawkins matchmaking classes she and the Sisterhood of Three held."

"Are you asking about who's relating to who?" Logan shrugged as he continued speaking. "Diagrams usually are drawings or lines connecting things together."

"Sorta of what I'm asking about." Dakota picked up a pen and pad off the nightstand. He laid them on the bed between them. He drew a circle, a triangle, a square and a V with dotted lines between their initials. "Some relate circularly. Everyone is involved with each other. Some are triangles due to the number involved. Quads are square-like. V relationships are where the middle of the V is the person the others are relating to but not to each other."

"I guess I'm the center point of the V." Cassandra tapped the V diagram.

"I prefer the circle or the triangle. Each relating to each other. Some get very specific and state solid lines are sexual involvement. I figure our diagram is up to us. Solid or dotted lines don't matter to me. We're in this together." Logan drew two intertwining circles next to the single circle. "We could add a third circle intertwining and intersecting the other two. One is you, Cassandra, relating to me. The other you and Dakota. The third is Dakota and me. Each of our circles intersects and intwines with the others."

"That leads to my fifth question, does a diagram of our relationship matter?" Cassandra pointed to the circle, triangle and intersecting circles. "Any of these could be us at any point. Is it anyone else's business?"

CHAPTER FOURTEEN

"Some will ask." Dakota shrugged. "If we formalize our bonding, a format may be necessary. I like trio. This leaves room for growth. If we want to add others at another point."

"*What?*" Cassandra pressed her lips tightly together. She flexed her hands. Add others? Deities on high, what was she agreeing to?

"It's okay." Dakota scooted closer to her. "Some group bondings decide to open to add others. Group marriages like the intertwining circles Logan drew. Mini packs forming a larger joint pack family. Complexities that I've heard of. Not something I am suggesting or contemplating."

"I don't think we need to diagram us right now." Cassandra handed Logan the question she held. "This is getting to complex for me."

Logan took the paper from her. "I agree. Let's go with the next question."

Dakota nodded. "What's the question?"

Logan unfolded the paper, gazed at it and smiled. "Let's stop the questions and go with what is our main concern." He held up the paper so Dakota and Cassandra could see it.

"I'm going first on this one." Cassandra pointed at Dakota and Logan. "Are you ready for one on one? Group stuff is okay to a point."

Logan spoke first. "I'm ready. We had one-on-one time with our nap. What about you Dakota?"

"Depends on what one on one is." Dakota stood and stretched. "Right now, it's probably sleep time."

Cassandra slowly exhaled. "Tonight I'd like the three of us to watch a movie after dinner. Popcorn and a comedy. Bedtime, I'll choose who sleeps with me."

"I'm in." Logan stood, leaning against the bed. "I saw a couple of books on the end table near the couch that intrigued me."

"Maybe a fire in the fireplace. If we can't watch a movie, we could take turns reading to each other." Dakota glanced at him and Cassandra.

"Sex happens with either of you when whoever I am sleeping with and I decide we're ready to go there." Cassandra stood and gathered the remaining slips of paper off the bed. "The rest of these questions can wait for another discussion."

She paused at the door. "I'm going to fold my clothes. Then start dinner."

"Logan and I will see what ingredients are available. We'll meet you downstairs in twenty minutes?" Dakota wrapped his arm around Logan's waist. "Lean on me. We'll take the stairs like we did on the way up. One at a time."

Cassandra watched Logan and Dakota make their way down the stairs. Dulce following them. She waited until they reached the bottom step. "Twenty minutes is good. See you in the kitchen. There might be some stew makings. Homemade biscuits too."

Dakota and Logan each gave her a thumbs up and continued toward the kitchen. Cassandra stuffed the questions slips in her jeans pocket and entered her bedroom.

She dumped the hamper on the bed and sat next to the pile of clothes. She picked the clothing item closest to her. A lacy black bra. She folded it in half and grabbed the next piece of clothing. Red silk panties. She folded them and set them next to the bra. She hadn't chosen her undergarments with sexual allure in mind. Or had she? Silk wore well and the feel of it next to her skin was. . .Cassandra mouthed the word. Sexy. The smooth material slid across her legs and up her hips, caressing her like a pair of loving hands would. Pictures from the catalog she'd ordered the garments from flashed through her mind. Models smiling and posing like they were attracting someone. For her, it had been Dakota or Logan in her dreams and a few of her fantasies. She folded several more clothing items without paying attention to what they were. Two questions claimed her thoughts. Was she hiding her sexual attraction or downplaying it? What if she walked into the kitchen and French-kissed Dakota and Logan? Was she ready to be that bold and announce her interest in sex with either of them later tonight?

Logan perched on the seat of the wheelchair. "Did we overwhelm Cassandra too much?"

Dakota leaned the crutches against the couch. "I don't know. Maybe some. We overwhelmed each other."

Logan settled back in the wheelchair. "Winging telling someone you're interested is not easy. No cut-and-dried responses. Can't predict an outcome."

"We did. We got the same answer from each of us. We're interested and are moving forward." Dakota sat on the arm of the couch. "Group dating is new for all of us."

Logan shook his head. "That's for sure. We make it up as we go along."

"Yep." Dakota stood. "I think I remember my Mam's baking powder drop biscuit recipe. I'll make those to go with dinner. What's your contribution?"

Logan wheeled toward the kitchen. "Depends on what's available. I think I saw some tapioca flour and pudding mix in one of the cabinets. A couple of eggs and some milk along with a cup of powdered cocoa or hot chocolate mix concoct a sweet cake. Simple and easy."

Dakota followed him into the kitchen. "Cinnamon butter for the biscuits. Your cake. And a stew or more soup sounds good. I wonder if there's enough of the soup left over to use as a starter for chicken stew."

"A couple of potatoes diced, a bit of onion, a garlic clove, and some chopped chicken plus mixed vegetables would do it. Flour to thicken the broth." Logan opened the fridge.

"Damn dude. I didn't know you could cook." Dakota took the onion and potatoes out of the vegetable bin on the counter.

"Rests on your definition of cooking. My mom made sure I learned quick and easy stuff like making leftovers stretch. Some I got from reading cookbooks. Haute cuisine not my thing. Simple and filling, I can manage." Logan set the bowl of leftover chicken soup on the table.

"You're cooking with my help. I had thought about beef stew. Chicken stew is good. I'll get the mixed vegetables out of the freezer." Cassandra took a bowl out of the cabinet near the door to the sunroom pantry door. Cold air swept into the kitchen, swirling past her as she opened the door and entered. The icy chill wound its way around Logan's legs and past Dakota toward Dulce. Dulce barked and growled, running out of the kitchen as if the air chased after her.

"If power goes out, we can put all the cold stuff out there." Logan chafed his arms and legs.

"Solar panels will keep us warm, lighted and watching the comedy you and Dakota picked out." Cassandra reentered the kitchen, quickly shutting the sunroom pantry door. "Frost on the screens, window panes and cold enough in there to freeze anything that ain't already froze."

Dakota took the bowl from her and placed it in the kitchen sink. "Getting dark outside. Dulce need another potty run before it gets too dark?"

"Yes. Turn on the backlight and set her on the step. She knows what to do from there." Cassandra put the bag of mixed vegetables in the fridge. "Found four chicken thighs. Going to take a bit to thaw them in cold water, then trim the fat off."

"I'm going out with Dulce for a moment. Make sure she gets done and come back in." Dakota tied his hikers and slipped his jacket on. "I'll put more deicer on the drive and walk. Be back in a few."

"Do you have the recipe on your cell phone?" Cassandra put the chicken in a bowl of water.

"Bits and pieces worth stashed somewhere. Every time I've made it, I've used whatever I had on hand. My mom called it surprise cake cuz you made it with what you had. Usually eggs, flour, sweetner, and butter plus some flavoring or pudding added to it."

"Grandma has one very similar she never wrote down. Swore she never makes it the same way twice." Cassandra laughed. "Granddad and I know better. He always asks for butterscotch surprise cake for his birthday."

"My Great Aunt Anne referred to it as the family courting recipe. Way to a person's heart is through their stomach. My brother and I expanded it to cooking for ourselves. Needed special recipes we could duplicate without calling Mom or Aunt Anne for advice." Logan held up three fingers. "First ingredients: Three eggs, three tablespoons melted butter, three cups flour."

Cassandra set a large mixing bowl on the counter. "Flour might be a problem."

"Nah, I saw the tapioca flour. Flavoring is the next ingredient. Three teaspoons of an extract or a quarter cup of cocoa or hot chocolate mix. Last item is sugar or powdered sugar."

"How big a baking pan do you need?" Cassandra flipped the page she was writing on.

"Square, rectangular, or even bundt will do." Logan pulled the pad to him. "Let's gather the goods and get this cake cooking."

Cassandra placed a wire whisk and bowl on the table. "I'll put the oven to preheat. You can get the eggs and butter. Do we need water or milk with this?"

Logan snapped his fingers. "I knew I forgot something. Milk if we don't use hot chocolate mix. Otherwise water. Two and a half cups warm water or chilled milk."

Dakota opened the back door, set Dulce on the floor and entered. "What smells so good?"

"Chocolate tapioca cake." Cassandra laid the thawed chicken thighs on the cutting board. "Logan's recipe is easier than I suspected."

Dakota hung up his jacket. "Snow is starting to fall again. Wind's died down. It's still pretty cold."

"Thanks for taking Dulce out." Cassandra cut the thighs in half and deskinned them. "I'll help you with your recipe after I put these thighs in the microwave."

"Where is Logan?" Dakota kissed Cassandra's cheek.

"Living room. Checking out the books. Seeing what taped movies I've got." Cassandra turned her lips puckered. Dakota brushed his lips over hers.

"What brought this on?" Dakota stepped back.

"I kissed Logan. Chocolate-covered lips taste very sweet when covered with cake batter." Cassandra put the glass baking dish holding the thighs in the microwave and set the timer for four minutes.

"Ah keeping things level." Dakota eased his hikers off.

"Not necessarily. Wanted to see if kissing each of you was as sweet as I remembered."

"Your kisses are as delicious as I remember them." Dakota put his moccasin slippers on. "Mam's baking powder biscuits have five ingredients. Baking powder, milk or water, eggs and flour plus a bit of sugar."

"Do you two need a chaperone?" Logan called out from the living room.

"Not any more than you did with your recipe and cooking time." Dakota walked to the living room door. "I think we can finesse the biscuit making as well as you did the cake making."

Logan laughed. "Okay, I'll keep busy working last Sunday's crossword puzzle."

Dakota retrieved the milk and eggs from the fridge. "Baking powder is the main ingredient along with the half-cup of sugar. Leavening agents mixed dry. Eggs beaten with a touch of milk and a pinch of salt. Slowly mix in with the baking powder and sugar. Adding a quarter cup of flour and milk plus a tablespoon of water to keep the mix wet until all ingredients are blended."

"Greased baking sheet or parchment paper?" Cassandra set the baking sheet on the table.

"Either. I prefer using a bit of butter to grease the pan. Browns the bottoms better. Spoon drop the biscuits onto the baking sheet and bake at three-fifty for fifteen to eighteen minutes." Dakota measured the baking powder and sugar into the bowl and stirred.

"Oven is preheating." Cassandra checked the microwave. "Thighs are almost done. Debone them and add some broth to the leftover soup plus the mixed vegetables plus the potatoes and onion Logan chopped up. Simmer for ninety minutes until stew is thoroughly heated."

"We could start our own cooking channel." Logan wheeled into the kitchen. "I found a couple of romantic comedy movies we could watch. Or we could do something else."

CHAPTER FIFTEEN

Cassandra pushed back from the table. The last question lay open on the table. Part way into the last canasta game, she'd dug the remaining questions out of her jeans pocket. Somewhere between the first canasta game, half a sleeve of munched crackers, and checking on the stew, they'd agreed to continue their prior conversation over dinner. Problem was each of them had drawn a question, opened it, read it and turned it face down on the table. The stove timer chimed again signaling the stew was ready. She glanced down at her question wondering how she was going to answer it. That would have to wait until after dinner and she hoped one of the romantic comedies they'd agreed to watch. She paused at the kitchen door. "Easiest way to do this is to dish up in here."

Logan started gathering the playing cards. "I'll clear the table."

Cassandra nibbled her bottom lip. Would Logan look at the questions or leave them turned down? She stepped back toward the table. She grabbed her question and stuffed it in her pocket. "Dakota, do the same with yours. Logan, you too."

Dakota shoved his in his jeans back pocket. Logan held his up. "Not easy to do with small pockets." He wadded up the slip, leaned on the table, rising slightly and pushed the slip into the small front pocket of his jeans.

"Thank you." Cassandra entered the kitchen. Dakota right behind her.

"If you don't want to answer more questions, we don't have to." Dakota leaned against the counter.

"Questions need answers. Answers can ignite more questions." Cassandra handed Dakota two potholders. "It's like learning a new thing. You gotta wing it sometimes. Or fake it until you understand better."

She set bowls, spoons and napkins on a serving tray. Next to them she placed the bowl of biscuits and cinnamon butter. "I'm sorry if this unnerves you and Logan."

"Can't speak for Logan." Dakota picked up the pot of stew. "Doesn't worry me. We're all in new territory. We're checking in a lot 'cuz we care. Nothing wrong with that."

"Thanks. I appreciate you understanding." Cassandra picked up the tray. "I'll come back for the ice water pitcher."

"Let Logan get it. Each of us is helping out." Dakota moved up beside her. "Ease the tension if we're each help out."

"Yeah." Cassandra exited the kitchen. "Logan, thanks for clearing the table. The pitcher of ice water is on the counter. Would you please get it?"

"You bet." Logan wheeled toward the kitchen. "Stew smells great."

"I forgot the ladle. Be right back." Dakota placed the stew middle of the table on top of the hot plate trivet Logan had put out as he cleared the table. He hurried into the kitchen. Slowing as he reached Logan.

"Hold up a moment." Dakota reached for the ladle. "Cassandra's question has her spooked. We're checking in lots. Maybe it's time to ditch the questions and talk about what's spooking each other."

"Honest feelings without getting defensive isn't easy." Logan pointed to the pitcher. "That is colder than I thought. I'll take the ladle. You carry the pitcher?"

Dakota handed Logan the ladle. "You're on."

Cassandra placed the tray on the credenza. She pulled her question out of her jeans pocket, read it, sighed and put it back in her pocket. Why did she fear answering the question? Or was asking it that left her anxious?

Sex, nudity, and . . . who was she kidding? She'd seen Dakota and Logan nude. Naked came to mind with her fantasies and dreams. Nude took on its own connotation. A sexy one given the blasted question she drew. How did she read a sensual laden question and not let her thoughts run. . .Thoughts were already flashing back to what she'd seen that morning. Dakota and Logan hadn't rushed to hide. Nor apologized multiple times. They were at ease with their nudity and put the incident behind them. Was her fear of them seeing her nude? Undressing in front of either of them?

"Cassandra, Logan and I . . ." Dakota entered the dining room first. He stopped speaking. His gaze met hers. He nodded. "Whatever the question is, let it go. We are at a point where we need to talk freely."

"I agree with Dakota." Logan wheeled into the dining room. "Let's talk while we eat."

Cassandra took the ladle, filled the bowls and placed them on the table. "The question is one we've danced around since last night."

Dakota poured water into the glasses, placed the pitcher on the table and pulled out the chair closest to him. "I'm going to name what I think are the items we're not naming. Sex, nudity, and open discussion about this."

Cassandra picked up her glass of water, drank a third of it and refilled her glass. "Obvious is out there."

Logan spread his napkin across his lap. "I had a hard on this afternoon sleeping with you. I own it. I didn't pursue things because we hadn't talked about it. Consent is a priority with me. Dakota could have walked in on us. Or vice versa if it were you and Dakota. Not fair to any of us if that had happened."

"I've fantasized about sex with you, Cassandra. I haven't pursued either because I'm not a screw-em-and-leave-em person. Pleasure, mutual consent and caring are important integral parts of physical and emotional intimacy for me. I'm a lover." Dakota buttered a biscuit, bit into it and chewed.

Who spoke next would point to where the discussion flowed. Dakota savored the tangy flowing, sparking his taste buds. Savoring the essence of each bite, the spices, taste and flavor of food enhanced his meals. Same went for his approach to lovemaking. The F word didn't fit his way of seeing or doing sex and wasn't part of his vocabulary.

"Comfort levels are important to intimacy. Logan and I need to know yours. Nudity isn't always part of sexuality or intimacy. Comfortable in your own skin and how you look are very important too." Dakota broke the rest of his biscuit up into his stew.

"I guess I'm next in this." Logan laid his spoon down. "I enjoy sex. Intimacy too. Emotional intimacy is so different than physical. I've felt connected to you from the moment we met. It was like my search was over. I didn't know my heart was searching."

"Searching?" Cassandra sipped her water, broke a piece off her biscuit and popped it in her mouth.

"Looking for someone. Listening to our heart isn't something we readily do." Logan held up his biscuit. "I get hungry. I look in cabinets seeing what is easy, quick and requires little work. Seeking the one is not easy if we aren't in touch with ourselves. Shapeshifters got two yammering at them."

Dakota pushed his empty bowl aside. "When the two unite, sparks are happening. Our wolves know. Reading auras is one of our magics. Some of us are better at it than others."

"When did you read mine, Dakota?" Cassandra pushed her biscuit along the bottom of her bowl, sopping up the last bits of broth and chicken bits. She cut the biscuit in two and ate half waiting for Dakota to respond.

"Second dance, the second Sadie Hawkins we attended. The one we attended together. No necessary introductions." Dakota chuckled. "We kept eyeing each other at the first."

Cassandra turned toward Logan. "And you, Logan?"

"Second full moon aka autumn blue moon Sadie Hawkins last year. We danced two slow dances. Dated for a bit. Each time I touched you, my wolf howled and growled, wanting to mark and mate you. Lots of cold showers that fall." Logan drank the rest of his water.

Cassandra pushed her bowl away from her. She toyed with her napkin, turning it back and forth. How did she explain what she felt and continued feeling each time she got near Dakota or Logan? Granddad said second sight ran in the family. Grandma talked about her dreamtime visions. Precognitive insights she called them. What had Granddad said about his psychic intuitions? Telepathic empath. Able to pick up on people's energy and thoughts. What Maggie called reading auras. Did she admit her possible supernatural abilities or was it a magic gene that was far back in Granddad's and Grandma's family?

"I can't explain why." Cassandra pushed back from the table. "I just know I felt similar."

"Similar how?" Dakota moved his chair closer to her.

"Warm tingling feelings like something embraced me. I wanted to touch each of you more after we danced. I dreamt of orange, purple and red colors."

Dakota laid his hand on her right hand. "The aura colors of love, seduction and attraction."

"Maggie says aura reading is seeing the colors outlining a person. It's like seeing their soul energy." Cassandra inhaled slowly. She glanced at Logan.

Logan nodded and wheeled closer to her. He laid his hand on her left hand. "We shapeshifters are dualities. Dakota and I are wolf and human, occupying the same physical realm. The energy we project is part of our living forces. A living partnership."

Cassandra exhaled. She entwined her fingers with Logan's and Dakota's. "There's a part of me that feels the energy in this room. The power that flows and pools together when we're like this."

Dakota let go of her hand and slid an arm around her waist. "There's a tale that soothsayers tell of a time when animals and humans co-existed. They could understand each other. Communicate with ease and a clear understanding of their part in the world. Balance and attentiveness to every living thing. Plants as well as animals and humans. Each needed the other to thrive. "

"I heard my family's version. Similar in many places. Communicating with our animal duality happens because of bites, magic trade-offs and powers-that-be seeing the balance of power is kept." Logan stood, placing both hands on the table. He shuffled closer to her until he was between her and the table. Balancing against the table, Logan slid his arm around her.

Cassandra glanced at Logan and Dakota. She slowly exhaled. "I'm going to ask a question that isn't part of the ones we came up with."

"Sure." Logan hugged her, pulled her chair to him and sat on it.

"Say what's on your mind." Dakota slid two chairs close to her. He sat in one and patted the other. "Take a seat."

Cassandra perched on the edge of the chair. "How do you feel about being the stars of a woman's fantasies?"

Logan opened and closed his mouth twice. He turned in the chair toward her. "Both of us at the same time?"

"Yeah, what he said." Dakota folded his arms across his chest.

Cassandra stood and angled her chair so she could see Dakota and Logan easier. She chafed her arms as she sat. "Not at the same time. Separate ones. Views like this morning. And more."

"I don't mind showing off my good looks, clothed or unclothed." Logan pointed to the wheelchair. "Push it closer. Numb ass permit focused conversations very well."

Dakota rose and pushed the wheelchair closer to Logan and the table. "This morning you got an eyeful. Hope you enjoyed it."

"I very much enjoyed the view. Thank you both." Cassandra ducked her head and looked back up. "I don't know if my naked view will thrill either or both of you."

Logan wheeled close to her. He laid his hand on hers. "Sweetie, there's more to attraction than physical. I look at you and I see a caring, genuine person who cares about the students she helps, her community and what she can do to help her neighbors. I got hard because I wanted to touch you and pleasure you. I want to be nude with you and naked with you emotionally as well as physically."

"I echo what Logan said." Dakota placed his hand close to hers on the table. "I've spent nights aching, wanting to pleasure you and I both."

Cassandra stood. She unbuttoned the first button of her top. "I guess it's time to find out."

CHAPTER SIXTEEN

"What are you doing?" Dakota pushed back from the table.

"Shucking my clothes." Cassandra unbuttoned two more buttons.

"Why here?" Logan wheeled up next to Dakota. "Why now?"

"Answers a whole lot of questions. I get it over with." Cassandra undid the last button.

"No passion? No desire?" Dakota moved closer to Cassandra. "What are you afraid of?"

"You letting fear drive?" Logan asked, moving up beside Cassandra. "If you're not interested, say so. Our friendships will survive."

Dakota raised his hand, palm toward them. Logan raised both of his palms toward Dakota, the other toward Cassandra. Dakota placed his palm against Logan's.

"Logan and I are ready to commit to you. Not because you're ready to strip for us." Dakota thrust his palm toward Cassandra. "We want more than a quick roll, a peep show and more than the sex."

"It's too soon for the L word." Cassandra glanced at both of them.

Logan shook his head. "Friends can love each other. We're more than friends in many ways. We're a family. We're on the verge of declaring it ourselves. I'm ready to commit too. I'm not scared to do this."

Cassandra faced Dakota. "You feel the same way?"

"Ready to declare us a family unit? Yes." Dakota started to lower his palm. "Question is are you?"

Cassandra slowly inhaled. Committing sounded ominous. Family of choice declarations. That didn't have a menacing tone to it. Since her grandparents retired and started traveling, loneliness filled more of her hours than she realized. Having Logan and Dakota here was. . .she exhaled, swiped her palms up her top and turned.

Warmth pooled around each of her wrists. Heat pulsed upward. Over and around her shoulders, sliding down into each palm and back to the source of the two palms tight to hers. Dakota's gaze met hers. Logan's as well. Dakota and Logan nodded as they glanced at each other and back to her.

Dakota stepped into the circle they formed, stopping when inches from her. "I claim you as part of my family. Part of the circle that surrounds my heart. Pulsates deep within my and my wolf's beings and hearts. I promise to honor and cherish you."

He turned slightly, facing Logan. "You are my brother. Our wolves share a bond no one can shatter. I claimed your friendship long ago. Our wolves may be from different packs. They knew they and us were a special pack. That bond is family that resides deep within my wolf heart and my human one. You are my brother and packmate now and always."

Logan gripped Dakota and Cassandra's hand, pulling him and the wheelchair into the center of the circle close to Dakota and facing Cassandra. He pressed his palms against Dakota's and Cassandra's as he spoke. "Cassandra, you are my and my wolf's heart choice. Our friendship binds us and entrusts us to each other. We claim you as family now and forever more."

Logan faced Dakota as best he could. "Dakota, you are the extra brother I never had. The friend who welcomed me from the first hello. You cared for me, even helped me through many of life's ups and downs. Our wolves bonded, forming our own unique pack. You and I are family. Pack mates now and always."

Cassandra pressed her palms tighter to Dakota's and Logan's. She and her heart could sort out their fears and worries later. Family and friends mattered. Those that claimed you as both were special. Especially the non-blood ones. Family of choice. Her choice and they chose her. Dakota's and Logan's spoke vows and claims were gifts. Gifts that shapeshifters bestowed on an elite few. The ones they trusted with their life, heart and inner animal's life.

"I, Cassandra," she began stepping into the circle until one foot touched Dakota's and part of her leg touched Logan's, "vow to honor your friendship, trust and family commitment and claim. I claim you both as pack mates, family members by choice and whatever else may come. This I swear now and always to you both. We are family."

Hands clasped the one next to them tightly. Heat pulsed across one palm. Rapidly passing over the next. Up arms and across the heart zone of each chest until it seared and sizzled its way around and over the next palm. Lips brushed Cassandra's cheeks. Her breathing slowed. Colors. . .bright vivid reds. . . deep aquamarine blues. . .mauves deep and rich in rose red edges pulsating as their center core ignited in purple and periwinkle hues.

Lips captured her earlobe, worrying it between the teeth the lips covered. Dakota's husky whisper scorched its way into her core. "No lust. No quick and done see you happening here. You're wanted. You're desired. When you're ready, pleasuring you is going to be delicious and worth the time building both of us to release. Maybe mutual release."

Cassandra blinked. The kaleidoscopic blaze of colors faded as her vision cleared. She gripped Dakota's hand as the dining room came into focus. "I need to sit down."

Logan wheeled closer to her. He patted his lap. "Sit here. I can hold you."

"Are you sure?" Cassandra pulled back from Dakota.

"Yes. The chair held Dakota and I okay." Logan grinned. "Learned to drive it better after running over Dakota's foot a couple of times."

"Tip of my slippers. No injuries or harm done." Dakota moved away from Cassandra, creating space between them. "Tripped over my two feet, leaned against the wheelchair, getting my footing. Damn near sat in his lap."

"Are you two safe to leave unchaperoned?" Cassandra started to step around the wheelchair. Logan caught her hand.

"It's okay to sit on my lap." Logan blew her a kiss and patted his lap again. "Please?"

Cassandra released Dakota's hand. "Okay, not for long."

Cassandra faced Logan, placed both hands on the arm pad closest to her, and gradually sat catty-cornered on Logan's lap. She could see Dakota and Logan easily. "Let me know when I get too heavy."

Logan leaned to her, his breath warming her ear. "You're not too heavy. You're delicious. I wanna make you squirm with passion. See you flush as you climax. I adore women with curves. You and your curves turn me on a lot."

Logan captured her lips as she turned her head. His hands softly cupped her face. Lips parted. Tongues met in the age-old mating dance. Logan retreated. She followed, savoring every nuance and taste. Cinnamon, bursts of chili powder and other flavors from the chicken stew. Logan slowly closed his lips and pulled back.

"*Wow*." Logan rubbed his lips together. "Don't get up too quick. I've got a hard on. Gonna be pretty conspicuous."

Cassandra ducked her head and nodded. Heat flushed over her. Dakota and Logan each showed her they desired her. Logan's evidence pressed against her buttocks. She looked at Dakota. Her gaze roved lower. She swallowed and gripped the armrest tighter as she rose. He was turned on? He reached down, tugging each of his jeans' pant legs and swiped his hands upward. He shrugged as he shoved his hands into his pockets. "Must of shrunk my jeans a bit, washing and drying them."

"No need to hide your desire." She stood and faced Logan and Dakota. Her taut nipples pebbled and pushed against her bra showing off their interest and desire-laden intoxicated state. "I'm not hiding mine very well either."

"I think we've moved past the what do we do when we get naked question." Dakota moved around the table and sat in his chair. "I'll add I'm not a voyeur. Threesomes don't thrill me."

"Thanks for letting me off the hook." Logan wheeled back to where his bowl and glass were on the table. He picked up the knife lying next to the chocolate torte. "Some say chocolate is an aphrodisiac."

"How about chocolate satisfies sweet tooth cravings? Nothing more." Cassandra sat in her chair.

Dakota pushed his bowl and glass to the middle of the table. He handed Logan a small dessert plate. "We could strip buck ass naked and wipe the chocolate all over each other then lick it off."

Logan pulled back the plate holding the first slice of cake. "One, you are not wasting my beautiful cake on lewd doings. Two, I ain't licking nothing off you. Kissing you or anything in that realm. You're not my type."

Dakota reached for the cake. "See what I put up with. Cassandra, we need you to balance these lust outbursts."

Cassandra covered her mouth. One muffled laugh, followed by another louder than the first sounded. Dakota winked and pulled the plate away from Logan. Logan shook his head, put a piece of cake on a plate and handed it to her. He grinned and quickly looked away. Cassandra took the plate and set it in front of her.

"I think both of you gotta work this one out on your own. Meaning neither of you are going to get your way. Dakota, I agree with Logan no lewd food things. Logan, you need to learn self-control. Me, I am going to enjoy my cake while you two behave."

"*Behave?*" Dakota and Logan blurted out almost simultaneously. Logan spurted and coughed, reaching for his partially full glass of water. Dakota picked up his fork, saluted each of them and began eating his cake.

Logan laid a slice of cake on his plate. "Ah, tastebuds look out. Deliciousness incoming."

Dakota laid his fork down after consuming several bites of his piece of cake. "Dude, hard to believe this was a dump cake recipe your mom coached you over the phone on."

Logan wiped his mouth, nodding as he laid his fork and napkin down. "Surprised me, too. Between her and my grandmother, I got a bunch of quick simple toss-together recipes every time I called either of them."

"How about some decaf tea or coffee to go with the rest of the dessert?" Cassandra pushed back from the table. "I'll put the rest of the torte in the fridge."

Dakota started staking their bowls and glasses. "Logan and I can help with the cleanup."

"Yeah. We can finish our cake and coffee or tea in the kitchen." Logan handed the cake and platter to Cassandra. "Dakota if you wash, I'll dry unless the dishwasher is ready to run."

"I appreciate you helping out." Cassandra gripped the cake platter tighter. Part of the question she drew was answered. Part of it wasn't. At some point, the remaining part needed answers. She knew there was one section that was exempt from the answer. The squeaky twin bed in the den.

"Dishwasher is almost full. These dishes will fill it." Dakota moved aside as he entered the kitchen. "Does Dulce need to go again?"

Logan wheeled in, carrying the water pitcher, empty soup pot, and ladle on his lap. "I'll rinse. Dakota, you load?"

"Wouldn't hurt to take Dulce out one more time. She ate and ducked under the end table. She's probably asleep." Cassandra set the cake platter on the counter. She placed the remaining half of the torte in a refrigerator storage container and clicked the lid closed. "I can take Dulce out."

"Let me do it, please." Dakota put the rinsed bowls and spoons in the lower half of the dishwasher. He reached for the rest of the rinsed dishes Logan held out to him. "I can pull on my hikers, jacket and hat quick and easy. It's getting Dulce ready that takes two."

Logan dried his hands on the dish towel Dakota handed him. "Cornering Dulce isn't going to be easy." Logan patted the wheelchair's sides. "Me and wheels will help out with that."

"Easier said than done." Cassandra closed the dishwasher and turned it on.

Dakota picked up his hikers. "Got an idea. I'll sit in the chair close to the end table and put my hikers on. I bet if I call Dulce, she'll bolt for the kitchen if Logan has the stairs blocked."

"What if she doubles back?" Cassandra laid Dulce's coat on the counter.

"Not if you're blocking the doorway once she enters the kitchen." Dakota started toward the living room. "Everybody take their places."

Cassandra shook her head. Dulce might surprise them all. The scamp could move fast when she wanted to. She picked up Dulce's coat and entered the living room.

"Dulce, Chuy's outside. Wanna go see him?" Cassandra sat on the couch. She hoped the barks she heard were Mrs. Abernathy and Chuy making his nightly potty walk down her driveway across the front lawn watering every tree or car tire he could reach.

Logan wheeled past the couch and turned, partially blocking the stairs. "Dulce, when you come back in, I'll have treats ready."

Dulce barked twice, coming partway out from under the table. She looked at Cassandra who held up her coat. Logan held up his hands.

Dakota walked over to the chair looked at Cassandra and Logan. Sighed and sat down. So much for working a unified plan.

CHAPTER SEVENTEEN

"Hey Dulce, how about you and me go outside? Go see Chuy?" Dakota pulled on his hikers and tied them.

Dulce took two steps toward him. He leaned down, holding out his hand. "Good girl. Come on, let's go outside."

The front door grate started humming. Wind blasted against the door, rattling it. Dulce turned and bolted toward the couch. Crap, twenty minutes chasing Dulce wasn't what he had in mind. A quick out to her doggie yard, a couple of piddle squats and a poop pile, and back in where it was warm and damn more inviting than chasing a pugnacious pug out from under an end table.

Cassandra leaned down, shaking Dulce's coat. "Come on sweetie. Quick out and bark at Chuy. Go potty and treats when you come back in."

Dulce backed up, barking. Dakota stood, moved toward Dulce. Logan wheeled closer to the couch. Cassandra shook the coat and patted the spot next to her. "Chuy isn't going to wait much longer. He doesn't like the cold either."

Dulce spun around, growled at him and Logan and sprinted toward the end table. Dakota took two strides to the left. Dulce cut to the right. Logan wheeled in front of her. More growls and barks sounded. Dulce backed up, cutting to the left this time. Cassandra stood, blocking the front of the end table.

"Look Dulce, you're going out. Chuy is going inside if you don't hurry. No treats if I have to carry you to the door." Cassandra tossed the coat on the couch. "Make up your mind."

Dulce scampered up to Dakota, sniffed boots and backed away growling. She ran over to Logan, barked at him and ran toward Cassandra. Dulce growled and barked twice, jumped on the couch and sat on her coat.

"If my wolf spoke dogese and could translate it efficiently, I might understand what that was all about." Dakota reached for the coat. Dulce growled, bearing her teeth more.

"Let me handle this." Cassandra tugged at the coat, grabbing Dulce's collar with her other hand. "You're going out. You'll see Chuy and go potty. Dakota is taking you."

Cassandra tugged harder, pulling Dulce toward her at the same time. Two quick tugs and a squirming Dulce lay on her side. Both of Cassandra's hands holding her down. "Grab her coat, Dakota. Let's get it on her. Logan, can you get her leash off the coat pegs, please."

"You bet." Logan wheeled into the kitchen. "Dakota, I think Cassandra and Dulce got a tag team match going. Tag your Cassandra's help."

Snarls, growls, and yipping sounded. Dulce squirmed, trying to pull her leg and paw out of Cassandra's hand. Teeth bared, she turned her head and went for Dakota's hand.

A deep growl sounded. Silence filled the room. Cassandra looked over her shoulder. Logan wasn't behind her. Another growl sounded, softer in volume. Dulce whimpered and went still. Cassandra looked at Dakota. He nodded.

"Let go and let me finish getting Dulce's coat on her." Dakota slid the coat over Dulce's head and body. He swiftly worked the coat around her body. He picked Dulce up under one arm and started toward the kitchen.

Cassandra followed Dakota into the kitchen. Wolf growls? From Dakota?

Dakota stopped near Logan. Cassandra tugged at her ear. More low-toned growls and high-pitched yips? Both men looked at her, smiled and faced each other.

Dulce yipped twice and barked. Dakota deposited her in Logan's lap. "All right scamp. Let's get you outside. I think Chuy is waiting for you."

A bark sounded outside the kitchen door, followed by scratches at the door. Dulce jumped off Logan's lap. Her leash trailing behind her. Logan high-fived Dakota. "Humans one. Dulce half a point."

"I'll be back in about ten minutes." Dakota zipped up his parka and pulled on his watch cap. Cassandra felt his gaze rove over her. Almost reaching inside, looking for the place to ignite her desire all over again.

Dakota reached down, scooped up Dulce and her leash, winked and opened the door. "Think you two can *behave*?"

Cassandra glanced at Logan, opening her mouth to answer. The closing door and its click sounded. Dakota hadn't waited for either her or Logan to answer.

"What's this behave?" Logan wheeled closer to her. "Ten minutes alone. I'm game if you are."

Logan winked, puckered his lips and leaned toward her. Cassandra glanced at the door again. She could hear Dakota talking to Dulce getting fainter. He trusted them to . . .behave? Who's definition? Her nipples tightened, pebbling against her bra. Maybe kissing Logan might—Nah, that wouldn't cool things down. Cooling things down wasn't precisely where her libido kept tugging her thoughts.

"Wouldn't it be easier if I sat on your lap again and put my arm around your neck?" Cassandra put both hands on the wheelchair arms.

"Sure would." Logan settled against the back of the chair. He patted his lap. "Your seat awaits."

Cassandra carefully settled on Logan's lap. His arm circled her waist, cradling her to him. "This is cozy and comfortable."

Logan's hot breath scorched its way around her ear as he whispered, "No sense wasting time." He caught her earlobe between his lips, worrying it with his teeth.

Heat flushed lower, reaching down her neck into the v of her top. Her taut nipples tightened more as Logan cupped her breast closest to him. "If I had the time, I'd taste these and nibble them like I did your ear."

Logan captured her nipple between his thumb and finger, squeezing, twisting and let go. Hand and cloth rustled over and across her swollen nipples and breasts. Logan's hand roved lower, tugging her top up until his hand lay on her bare stomach. "Now if you keep trembling like that, I'm going to have to report our behavior."

"I'm not supposed to tremble and quiver?" Cassandra turned to see Logan better.

"Easy on the moves darlin'. Easy. Explaining wet spots isn't going to help." Logan angled his head. "Wasting no more time. Kiss me."

His lips brushed against hers. Lightly, then firmer. Tips of tongues met in the age-old dance of taste, pull back and taste again. Logan slid his arms loosely around her waist. Both hands lay close to the small of her back, rubbing up and down each time their tongues touched. Much more and she'd. . .

"Come on Dulce. Chuy said good night. Mrs. Abernathy shared cookies and some of Chuy's treats with us." The click of the back door opening sounded.

Cassandra dropped her arms. Her hands slid down Logan's chest stopping close to his heart. Swift heartbeats pressed against her palms. Each swell of his chest as he inhaled and exhaled accented the lively beats. Further evidence of her effect on Logan nudged her bottom. She turned Logan on.

She carefully raised her hands, placed them on the wheelchair's arms and whispered. "I think I best stand up. Misbehaving I enjoyed."

"I agree." Logan nodded toward the door. "Dakota probably knows we were doing our definition of behaving."

"Damn that wind is cold. The temperature is dropping. Golds and reds dotting the sky as the sunset." Dakota set two plates on the counter. "Cookies from Mrs. Abernathy. Pork slices from your neighbor across the street. Thanks for shoveling their walk."

Dulce ran inside, stopped, shook the accumulated snow off her and started toward the living room.

"Hey scamp. Remember the treats?" Dakota shut the door and started taking his jacket off. "You want them. You gotta behave. Unlike a few people in the room were probably doing."

"Spying on us?" Logan asked. He tightened his hold on Cassandra.

"Why would I?" Dakota hung his jacket up and turned. "Behaving is personally defined. Did you enjoy your behaving?"

Dakota winked, walked over to Cassandra and Logan, leaned down and thoroughly kissed Cassandra. Lips captured each other. He worried Cassandra's bottom lip slightly with his teeth and broke off the kiss. Dakota stepped back. "I enjoyed my behaving just now."

Cassandra tried to stand. "I-I." She tried to swallow. Her throat constricted. Her tongue refused to move. Dryness enveloped her mouth as if a California Santa Ana wind whipped up over and through her. Her knees refused to cooperate. She slapped her hands down on the wheelchair's armrests, catching herself before she dropped like a heavy stone back on Logan's lap. "S-sorry. I-I don't know what's wrong with me."

Dakota clasped her hand between his. "You're okay. Your shields are down. Logan's and my wolves Qi meshed with yours. Life forces melded and mated."

"What if I'm not ready for that?" Cassandra rose with Dakota's help.

"Our earlier declarations bond us. Make us family. Logan's and my wolves are your guardians. They are marking you and taking on your scent. Are you now saying you're revoking what you said earlier?" Dakota released her hand. Logan released her other.

"Please forgive me. I'm trying to understand something I'm unfamiliar with." Cassandra grabbed Dakota and Logan's hands. "Your explanation makes sense. I've got a lot to learn."

"All of us have a lot to learn. Learn about each other more. Learn how to get along as a family." Logan squeezed her hand and let go. "For me, no harm, no foul. Our declarations are amongst us."

Dakota tugged her to him. "Declarations and vows are not the same unless they are spoken in a bonding ceremony before a matchmaker and duly recorded. We're not there unless we unanimously agree to that level."

"Like Logan said, no harm, no foul?" Cassandra hugged Dakota and stepped back.

"Correct." Dakota filled the electric kettle with water and turned it on. "Let's put our apprehensions aside for a moment. Are we drinking tea or coffee?"

"Herbal tea for me." Logan stretched. "I need to stand and move a bit. I'll do that once we're back at the table."

"I need to use the restroom. I'll be back in a moment." Cassandra hurried toward the half bath. "There's a box of chamomile tea in the cabinet. Honey's next to it."

Dakota set three mugs on the counter along with the box of tea. He faced Logan. "We keep dancing around the edge of what if. Around the I'm not ready. Voicing our interest and attraction. How do we move forward?"

"Depends on where forward is for you. What is it you want to accomplish?" Logan took three spoons out of the drawer. "Hand me the honey pot. I'll take the cookies, spoons and honey pot into the dining room."

Dakota unplugged the kettle as it started whistling. He handed the honey pot and bag of cookies to Logan. "Forward is moving beyond being fearful of attraction and desire. Moving into trusting each other to speak freely. Possibly a bit soon for a lot of that. Cassandra's pheromones say she's interested. Very interested. Her aura is sparking mauve, blue and yellow. Love colors. Not saying we're there yet."

"I agree. Caring is definitely present." Logan nodded toward the closed bathroom door. "Perhaps it's up to us to break the ice. Tell her what we want. We each want to sleep with her. Sex only happens by mutual consent."

Dakota picked up the mugs and kettle. "Consent includes not pushing decisions by anyone. Even you and I."

Cassandra cracked the bathroom door open. Two things came to mind as she washed and dried her hands. Each of them was worried about upsetting the others. Mutual consent mattered to each of them. One last item rose to the top of her immediate list. Would either Dakota or Logan feel left out if she decided to sleep with either of them? Sex was lurking in the foreground as well. That was item that was between her and who she slept with. The idea of sleeping alone no longer intrigued her.

She combed her fingers through her hair, took a deep breath and slowly exhaled. She pretty much knew what her heart said, what her psyche encouraged her to do, and what her calm stomach silently said. Time to step over the line and disclose feelings had come.

Cassandra opened the box of tea, put two bags in each mug, and sat down. "I need to say something."

Dakota filled his mug, slid the kettle to her, and broke a cookie in half. "Sure. Go ahead."

Logan pushed his mug next to hers. "Fill mine, please. I want to hear what you need to say."

CHAPTER EIGHTEEN

Cassandra filled Logan's mug, set the kettle down, and put her spoon in her tea. She stirred for a few moments, added some honey and stirred the tea more. She picked up the other half of Dakota's cookie. "Each of us is part of the group. Individual needs, wants, and desires. Couples happen. Someone is left as a single. I'm worried about how either of you are going to feel if I said I want to sleep with one of you and not both."

Dakota laid his cookie half down. "First, Logan and I are not interested in each other sexually. Second, compersion is sharing the joy your friends and bond members feel. Taking joy in their joy. Because I trust Logan and he is my friend and chosen family member, knowing he and you are enjoying your time together, however spent, brings me joy."

"What he said. I see it this way. I care for you and Dakota. I'm happy he's having time with you and you with him. That brings me joy. If I am jealous or envious, then I need to own it and figure out why. Sometimes you gotta talk things out. Like now." Logan sipped his tea. "Ah hot and sweet. Just like our conversation."

Cassandra nibbled on her cookie. Logan and Dakota said they were okay with her spending time with each. First night would be with. . . she laid her cookie down. "Just because I sleep with you doesn't mean sex is happening."

"Understood," Dakota replied.

"Same here." Logan broke off part of his cake with his fingers. "Whoever you decide to cuddle with tonight. May they and you find peaceful restful joyous sleep."

"I broke the ice on sleeping with Logan this afternoon. I'd like to continue exploring that tonight." Cassandra looked down, waiting for Dakota to start objecting.

"I'm good with your choice." Dakota held up his mug. "Here's to learning more about each other as time permits."

Logan picked up his mug. "To learning more about each other."

Cassandra smoothed her hands across her jeans. She reached for her mug. "Dakota, how long is the jail closed for?"

"Remainder of the storm and possibly longer. Depends on when repairs can begin and finish. Why?" Dakota drank more of his tea.

"Time to get to know each other together as three." Cassandra raised her mug. "Here's to the time we have together now. Time for each of us after the storm, together, individually and as couples."

"Yeah, buddy time for Logan and me. You time with each of us individually." Dakota touched his mug to hers.

"Time to decide if we declare a Sadie Hawkins Full Moon match." Logan touched his mug to hers, then Dakota's. "Think three weeks is enough time?"

Cassandra set her mug down. "Maggie said once that declaring intent is required. Is that before or after the full moon?"

"We can check once we decide if we want to take this further." Dakota popped part of his cookie in his mouth and chewed.

Logan picked up his fork. "I can eat cookies later. Late night snack if needed. Not often I get to savor my chocolate dump torte. Too much to make for one person."

"Have we cleared the angst and fear waiting to pounce on any of us?" Cassandra cut into the remaining portion of her cake. She slowly raised her fork full of cake.

Dakota crumbled the other part of his cookie on top of the cake. "Punctured the balloon that was ready to burst for sure."

Logan laid his fork on his empty dessert plate. "Let's finish up here. Check the weather and figure out where we want to go from here while we're together. Sound good?"

Cassandra and Dakota put their forks on their empty plates, wiped their mouths, and held up their palms. One of theirs pressed against the other. Each held their other palm to Logan. Logan pressed his tight to theirs.

Dakota spoke first. "Tonight begins the intimacy of our declarations. I am good with figuring out what we want after checking the weather report. Cassandra, your thoughts?"

Cassandra nodded. "I agree. Our intimacy levels deepen with our declarations tonight. A new phase of beginning and learning."

Logan spoke last, rounding out the circular agreement between them." Let tonight bring us understanding. Mutual learning. And clarity that permits us to deepen our friendship and family commitment."

"My great grandma taught me sharing energy is key to fortifying the bond you make with others. She showed me that it didn't matter if they were blood family, extended family or part of the multiperson pair bonding." Dakota clasped Cassandra and Logan's hands. "Sending energy around the circle three times right and three times left repeating the words as you gazed into the person's next to you eyes 'I declare you my family' synced the bond and the power that the bond emulated."

"I'll start." Logan squeezed Cassandra's hand as he looked at her. "I declare you family."

Cassandra looked to her left at Dakota, squeezed his hand, stating, "I declare you family."

Dakota looked to his left. Logan readily met his gaze. Dakota squeezed Logan's hand. "I declare you family."

The circle repeated two more times, left to right. Ending where it started with Logan. "This time Cassandra, you start."

Cassandra turned toward Logan, clasping his hand she repeated her earlier declaration. "I declare you family."

Logan repeated his declaration to Dakota as before. Round the circle three times to the right this time. Again ending back where they started with Cassandra.

"Dakota, what if we repeat the declaration again. This time our hands and arms are intertwined as we repeat the declaration together. Maggie said she'd witness family bondings done that way." Cassandra moved her chair closer to Logan.

"Yes, that is another way. I've witnessed such unions for legal purposes. Not that we're going there right now." Dakota stood and pulled his chair closer to Cassandra and Logan.

Logan looped his arm around Cassandra's and Dakota's arms. He clasped each of their hands. Cassandra and Dakota did the same with their opposite arms and hands.

"How about this time after we repeat our declaration in unison, we both kiss Cassandra on the lips at the same time?" Logan asked.

Dakota nodded. "Yes, action backing up our declaration. I like that. Cassandra?"

"I'm ready to go there. Taking us to the next level. Let's do it." Cassandra wet her lips and rubbed them together. "On the count of three."

"One," Logan called out.

"Two," Dakota said in an equally loud clear voice.

"Three," Cassandra stated, no quivers or hesitations in her voice and tone.

In unison, they vowed their declaration again. Logan wheeled tight to Dakota and her. He stood as best he could with their help. Dakota slid an arm around her waist pulling her closer to Logan and him. Two sets of lips pressed light kisses on her cheeks, working their way across her face until they met at her lips. Breaths mingled, warmed faces and lingered as the heat and passion of the moment loitered as if their combined heat and focus on each other merged into one moment of unified thought and being.

Logan dropped into the wheelchair. "Sorry. Between my numb ass and throbbing ankle. Focusing on sexy thoughts—it ain't easy."

Dakota stepped back. "Be truthful. It damn well ain't happening right now."

"You gonna be around to keep score later?" Logan grinned and winked.

Cassandra glanced at both of them, shrugged and picked up her dishes. "I'm going to catch the weather report. There's dishes to take care of."

Five minutes later, the hourly weather report chime sounded as they washed and dried their dessert dishes.

"For a person who usually doesn't mind winter," the weather reporter began, pausing before he continued. "*This white stuff can stop right now!*"

Background chuckles from the newscaster could be heard. The weather reporter sighed. "Yeah, six to eight more hours of possible snowfall. Current totals are eighteen inches plus in Sylvan Valley, close to the mountains. Twelve to fourteen outside of town here in Cauldron Falls. Wouldn't be so bad if the wind died down and the cold blast from the north zigzagged back to where it came from. *The frigged north pole!*"

A buzz and crackle sounded as the newscaster started speaking. "Gotta bring Stu in and thaw him out. Trying to do the weather report outside is, let's say, like walking into a restaurant walk-in cooler not quite buck ass naked."

More crackles and buzzing sounded. A different voice sounded and another announcement aired. "We now return you to our regular programming. Polka Music Hour."

Cassandra quickly turned off the radio. "Sounds like Stu, Peter and Max got caught by the censors."

"That or the sponsor couldn't wait any longer." Logan chuckled. He hung the damp towel on the oven door handle. "Not that polka music gets a big draw except at the Octoberfest in Sylvan Valley."

Dakota smirked. "We could have a polka dance contest."

Logan tapped his ace bandage lightly. "Yeah, right and I get to see how many times I kick my ass as I try those fancy turns and footing. I don't think I'll join in."

Cassandra put the plates and utensils away. "We know we've got a while longer before the storm breaks. Do either of you need to check in with your offices?"

"Tomorrow is soon enough for me. My office knows I'm out due to my ankle." Logan wheeled toward the living room.

Dakota shook his head. "Only person above me is the mayor. He told me hole up and don't sweat things. Jail is closed. On campus security knows where to reach me and him if needed."

"I doubt anyone is attempting to compete with Stu being out in this." Logan turned around as he reached the kitchen door. "Watch a movie or talk more?"

Dakota pointed to the kitchen wall clock. "It's a little after ten. Been a long day."

"Three canasta games is enough for me. I'm not quite ready to sleep." Cassandra covered her mouth as she yawned. "I don't think I could stay awake through a movie."

Logan yawned. "That's catchy. We're not quite ready to sleep. We need to decide who's sleeping where."

"We decided that already." Dakota dropped into the chair closest to the couch. "The question is, do I mind sleeping with Cassandra in the same bed you slept with her in? Or vice versa? Does Cassandra mind?"

"Why does this have to be difficult?" Cassandra sat on the couch. Her arms folded tight across her chest.

"Feelings. Jealousy. That green-eyed pain-in-the-ass emotion. Preferences." Dakota leaned forward, resting his hands on the arms of the chair. "I prefer to sleep with you without knowing Logan has slept in the same sheets with you. Sex is another thing."

"Sex?" Cassandra rolled her eyes and sighed. "Logan, get your feelings and thoughts tossed in here."

"First, I agree with Dakota. Clean sheets for our night or nights together." Logan wheeled close to the coffee table and turned, facing her and Dakota. "We got condoms. STD talks are necessary. And in the morning if we're in your bed, I help you strip the bed so you can make it up fresh."

Cassandra lowered her arms, put her feet on the couch and leaned back against the couch arm. "I'm going to say my feelings. Then we'll start figuring out where the midpoint is."

"That's important." Dakota rose, walked over to the couch and sat next to Cassandra. "Logan and I want to know what you're thinking and feeling."

"True. We're in this together. We've got to hear each other out. Check in with each other." Logan wheeled closer to the couch.

Cassandra lowered her arms, flexed her hands and spoke. "The twin bed in the den is out. Second, Logan and I in his room tonight. Dakota, you're in mind when it's you and me. All the beds get changed first of the week."

Dakota and Logan nodded, motioning for her to continue.

Cassandra pressed her hands against her legs and continued speaking. "Since I haven't been seeing anyone, there's no STD issues. I got a physical and GYN check up a couple months ago. Nothing wrong. STD tested to be sure. Clear there."

Dakota leaned over, hugged her and kissed her cheek. "Thank you for laying it out there. Not easy to do."

Logan clasped her hand and squeezed. "Glad to know you're healthy overall. I'll go next. Doc at ER checked me out thoroughly. No issues as you saw this morning. Quarterly STD testing clear and no other health concerns than this." He pointed to his ankle. "Oh, need to add, not seeing anyone either until now."

"My turn and then I'm turning in. Logan, I'll help you up the steps. Let me know if you wanna shower or wash up before bed." Dakota stood and stretched. "I'm STD-free. Recent check-up with doctor for quarterly health rating for job. I'm not seeing anyone up til now."

Logan let go of Cassandra's hand. "A wash-up and turn-in sounds. Good. Where are the condoms?"

"Is that the box you tried to hide in the kitchen?" Cassandra stood.

"I took it upstairs last night. Figured easier to find if needed close to where the action is or would be." Dakota retrieved Logan's crutches off the dining room table. He walked over to the bookcase and picked up a book. "Thumbing through the book, a couple of short stories caught my attention."

Logan took the crutches and stood as best he could. "How about we read one together cuddled in my bed after we each get ready for bed?"

"I'm game." Cassandra started up the stairs. "I'm going to take a quick shower and meet you in Logan's room."

Dakota faced Logan. "Don't squeak the bed too loudly. I plan on sleeping, not keeping count of how many times, okay?"

Logan looked down and back up. "Dang, you gotta stop reading my mind. You might blush if you do."

Dakota laughed and shook his head. "We might be thinking the same thing. You wanna say out loud what we're thinking? See who blushes first? The reddest?"

CHAPTER NINETEEN

"Well scamp, it's you and me tonight. Not much room in this bed." Dakota set Dulce on the den's twin bed along with the book of short stories. Dulce ran up and down the bed digging up the ends of the top blanket until they were in a pile that she nosed her way under until only her curly tail stuck out.

Dakota shucked his jeans and shirt. He sat down on the bed, picked up the book, and ran his thumb over the slip of paper marking the last short story he, Cassandra and Logan had read together. The short story idea had turned into each of them reading one of their choice. Three stories later, between yawns and good night hugs, he called official tuck them in time. Cassandra asked who was tucking him in. Dakota laughed and picked Dulce up off the bed, named her his tuck-in partner. He laid the book on the nightstand. He stood, his hands reaching for his briefs' waistband.

Did he shuck them? Sleeping nude like he'd done the first night. Or—Logan and Cassandra were probably nude and trying to quietly pleasure each other. Nothing to get angry about. He and Logan had partial tents happening in their jeans most of the evening. Dakota gripped his briefs waistband. Did he go in and shower? Attempt some relief while soaping and rinsing?

Dulce rustled the blanket turning around and settling down again with her face peeking out from under the blanket. Dakota doubted she'd stay with him all night. Cassandra wanted to leave Logan's bedroom door open. Giving Dulce the run of the rooms. He didn't doubt the scamp would try to worm her way between Logan and Cassandra given the chance to. Closing the bedroom door behind him as he exited would permit Logan and Cassandra privacy and hopefully uninterrupted sleep.

Dakota folded the blankets back. Tossed the afghan Cassandra had given him last night for extra warmth on the bed, smoothed it out and shoved his briefs off. He tossed them on top of his jeans and shirt. He laid down, pulled the covers over him and turned on his side. His eyes closed as his breathing slowed. Images of Cassandra cuddled between Logan and him as they read played back as sleep enveloped him. Her head resting on each of their shoulders as she read. The pleasant happy moments replayed as REM sleep drew him deeper into its embrace.

Logan yawned, wincing as he tried to roll on his side. His hips and calves echoed his ankle's pings. ER doctor had warned him about this. "Hope the storm blows out of here by Wednesday. Would be nice to see the doctor and get the okay to start using the boot more."

Cassandra snuggled closer to him. "Are you in pain?"

"Not much. Tendons tighten up if I lay in one position for too long." Logan flexed his good ankle and calf. "Help me sit up so I can massage my calves."

Cassandra scooted away from him, tossed off the covers and stood. "Did you bring your pain meds upstairs when we came up?"

"Took one with dinner. Massaging my calf and thigh helps some." Logan pushed the covers off him. He rolled onto his back, raised his wrapped ankle and winced again. He reached for his knee. "Tightness and twinges are running up the back of my leg. Hip is throbbing."

"Can you straighten your leg out?" Cassandra briskly rubbed her hands together. Friction created heat and heat was one way of soothing muscles. Knotted pressure points pulsed enzyme signals that set off other close by muscles and tendons to knot up as well.

"A bit." Logan massaged his thigh. "Blasted charlie horse won't unknot."

"Can you turn over?" Cassandra sat on the edge of the bed. "I'll help you turn over."

"Not easily." Logan clasped her hand. "It's going to take a couple of moves to do it."

"That's okay." Cassandra clutched Logan's other hand. "Roll toward me as much as you can."

Logan rolled on his side facing her. He tugged the waistband of his briefs. "Might flash you."

"Not a problem." Cassandra kneeled on the bed. "I'll massage your calf a bit."

She rubbed her hands together again, placed the heels of her hands on Logan's thigh and rubbed briskly.

Logan grimaced twice and held up his hand. "It's helping. I need to pull my briefs up or off. They're bunching up around my balls."

Cassandra reached for the brief's waistband. "Probably easier to get them off. Leave em on and bunching up will happen again."

"No flashing this time." Logan gripped the waistband with both hands and shoved them lower. "Mutual strip and bare it?"

"I offered that earlier with you and Dakota." Cassandra tugged the leg of Logan's briefs. Was he really ready to bare it all for her?

"You did. Now it's one on one. Are you ready to be vulnerable physically and emotionally with me?" Logan tugged his briefs lower. "I'm ready."

"How about we strip at the same time?" Cassandra covered Logan's hands with hers. "I'm game if you are."

Logan gawked at her for several moments. "There's always that first moment. Are you doing this because you're ready or refusing to let fear decide for you?"

"Fear got left on the back step. Dulce and Chuy chased it away." Cassandra grabbed the legs of Logan's briefs with one hand. The hem of her nightgown in her other. "On the count of three. . .THREE!"

Cassandra tugged the leg of Logan's briefs as low as she could. She let go of Logan's briefs and with both hands, pulled her nightgown off, flinging it away from her.

Logan tried to swallow once—twice. Cassandra, nude from the waist up, sat on the bed grinning at him. Her arms were at her sides. No ducking her head. Not even a tinge of blush colored her cheeks or neck—his gaze roved lower. Was she completely naked? Naked sounded risqué and mischievous. There was nothing naughty about them being nude or partially nude. They were here, nude by mutual consent. He tried to sit up. If Cassandra was nude, he needed to catch up.

Cassandra stood and walked around the side of the bed. Logan opened his mouth. Words failed him. His fantasies paled compared to the reality in front of him.

Cassandra's breasts jiggled some as she moved. Natural movement. Nothing played up. Their fullness and pink nipples seized his focus. Delicious like red raspberries awaiting his taste. He pressed his lips together, trying to retain his tongue and not blurt his thoughts out. His gaze roved lower. Past Cassandra's waist. Lower until her pubic hair came into view. No evidence of waxing.

Trimming perhaps. He'd know for sure when he went in for a taste. Logan looked up.

Cassandra smiled. "Need help with your briefs?"

Logan shrugged. "Not turning down help. You offering?"

Cassandra kneeled on the bed. "Could be."

The mattress dipped, moving him closer to Cassandra. Logan worked his briefs down past his hips as best he could. He rolled onto his back and lifted one leg. "I'll leave these to your attention and care."

Cassandra tugged the briefs down as far as she could. "You gonna have to roll on your side. Bare your ass if you want these off."

Logan closed his eyes and opened them. "Never let it be said I'm uncooperative."

Cassandra drew back her hand as Logan rolled over. Playful swat on the ass might stir up trouble. She wasn't kinky. She doubted Logan was. Some people might take a swat as a sign of kink play starting or turn things off. Neither was her intent. She placed her hand on Logan's hip and slid his briefs down closer to his knees. "Almost got the sides even."

"I'll turn over to even the progress out." Logan rolled toward her.

"Actually, on your back one more time lifting up each leg will get them down and off." Cassandra moved to the foot of the bed, kneeling on the mattress again. "Can you scoot down to me?"

"I can try." Logan grinned and added. "I'm glad this isn't a threesome. We'd be laughing so hard. Nothing sexy would happen."

Cassandra smirked. "Shared laughter can be sexy. You are sharing intimate moments with loved ones."

She looked away. Her thoughts hadn't included the L word. She inhaled slowly as Logan began making his way down the mattress to her. His cock jiggled every time he moved. His pubic hair covered his groin.

"Keep looking at me that way and you might get a surprise." Logan moved closer to her.

Cassandra looked up. "Not planning on eating you up. Just a taste."

She wrapped her fingers around Logan's cock, leaned down and flicked her tongue twice across the tip. "Salty. Tasty. I need another taste."

"Before you do, can you get these off me?" Logan pointed to his briefs. "Distracts from things."

"Certain distractions not permitted." Cassandra kissed Logan's cock and let go. "Definitely going to need a few tastes."

Logan lifted one leg. Cassandra worked the briefs down his leg and slowly over his wrapped ankle. He lowered his leg. He raised his other leg, shaking it trying to work his briefs over his knee. "Thanks. Kiss and taste all you like with this blasted chastity contraption off."

"More than a taste!" Cassandra yanked the briefs down his leg and flung them over her shoulder. "Mutual tasting?"

"Taste each other? *Sure.*" Logan stroked his cock up and down, fondling his testicles on the downward stroke before heading back upwards. "Leisurely tasting is awesome. Tonight I won't last that long. I want inside you. Feel your pleasure happening."

Cassandra squirmed and shivered. Last person to look at her with desire got up and left once she undressed. Finding her confidence and breaking the circle of self-doubt took time and healing. There was no doubting the look in Logan's eyes and his words. His desire oozed out and over him, reaching out to her. His erection solidly showed his desire. His acknowledging her pleasure mattered—her nipples hardened, her clit swelled. Was it possible to orgasm on energy and words alone?

She stretched out beside Logan. Her feet near his head and his feet near her head. Logan snuggled closer to her. He laid his leg across her waist as he trailed his fingers up and down her leg.

"Darlin', let me go first. You deserve some TLC. If your nipples match your clit, you are swollen, needing a few kisses and massages right here." Logan licked the tip of his finger, slowly inserted it between her labia lips and stroked across and around her clit, applying pressure in between strokes.

Two strokes, followed by a third and a fourth each slow or fast. Logan leaned closer to her, resting his head on her thigh. With his other hand he parted her labia lips, puckered his lips and blew on her taut throbbing clitoris. He moved tighter to her.

Cassandra clutched the blanket in both hands. Pressure, release, and the cool air lowering the fire in her briefly before Logan started stroking and blowing again. How much more build-up could she take? "No tease." Cassandra jerked as Logan's hands cupped her ass pulling her snugger to him.

"No teasing, Darlin'. Getting you ready for this." Logan repuckered his lips. Slid his hands up Cassandra's hips, across her to the apex of her legs until his fingers parted her labia lips. He ducked his head, sticking out the tip of his tongue and flicked it across her clitoris. Fast quick licks followed by slower longer ones until he suckled her clitors between his lips. Rapid licks and sucking commenced. Her wetness flowed past his lips and onto his tongue. What he'd read was apparently true. What sweets a woman consumed added to her internal sweetness. Deities, she tasted like freshly churned cream, a bit salty and sweet.

CHAPTER TWENTY

Logan slowed his licking. Cassandra licked around his sensitive head, sucking him between her lips and . . .Logan shook. Each of them waltzed along desire's lacy edge closer to the leap into the pinnacle of—Logan cupped Cassandra's face. "We're too close to orgasming. Gotta slow down."

Cassandra gently pulled her arm out from under Logan's. Putting her hands on the bed, she leveraged her chest from between his legs. "You ok to move your ankle?"

"Take hold of my calf. Don't want to chance a muscle spasm." Logan raised his ankle off her waist.

Cassandra ducked her shoulder. "Rest your foot on my arm. As soon as I'm clear of your head, I can turn and help you with your leg and ankle."

They unwrapped their limbs from each other. Cassandra reached up, supporting Logan's ankle with her arm. "Almost there."

Logan slowly rolled onto his back, lowering his ankle at the same time. Cassandra shifted to her right, sliding her leg over his leg. Her mons brushed against his cock, reigniting desire's slowly diminishing flame.

"Looks like part of you needs a couple of kisses." Cassandra slid her tongue over and around him as she cupped his balls.

"Much more and I am going to explode." His hips jerked up off the bed each time Cassandra took him in her mouth, tasting him with her tongue. He grasped Cassandra's arm. "Want to explode inside of you. Condom please."

Cassandra tasted Logan one more time and slid his cock out of her mouth. She picked up the condom packet off the bed, opened it and clasped Logan in her hand. "Whose putting it on?"

Logan held out his hand. "This time best, let me. Next time you can, ok?"

Cassandra handed Logan the condom. "I'll steady you."

Logan eased the condom down over his cock head and onto his shaft until his fingers touched Cassandra's. She unhurriedly let go one finger at a time. Trailing each down him and across his balls. His balls tightened to him, swelling each time Cassandra fondled them. "I prefer to share an orgasm deep inside you. I'm very close if we keep prolonging things."

"On our sides or me on top?" Cassandra withdrew her hands. "Either is easy on you."

"Honey, I'm not going to last much longer." Logan checked the condom's placement. "You on top is best right now."

Cassandra lay beside Logan. No space between them. "Put your hand on my hips as I straddle you."

She rolled on her hands and knees. Across Logan's stomach bit by bit, she slid her hand. Warmth reached up, dragging its tendrils tentatively over her palm, nudging its heat forth until both mingled mixing flashes of desire's hunger exploding again.

Placing her hands on the bed close to Logan, Cassandra pushed up creating a small space between her and Logan. She slid one leg between Logan's, close to his groin.

"Darlin', keep going. I feel the heat rolling off you onto me." Logan brushed his hand against her pubis. "A bit more and I'm inside you where I need to be."

Cassandra straddled Logan's hips, clasped him in one hand and guided him into her. Full, flesh to flesh, and she rocked toward him and back.

Logan groaned, closing his eyes. Heat, snugness, and ripples surrounded him. He countered Cassandra's movement. Forward to her backward and reverse. Covering her breast with his hand on her next forward sway, he captured her nipple between his fingers. Wetness coated his fingers close to Cassandra's mons. Sliding two fingers between her labia lips, he stroked her taut clitoris. Back and forth, picking up speed as she tightened around him.

"So clo-close." Cassandra stopped rocking. "Almost there."

Logan let go of Cassandra's breast and nipple. If his balls swelled anymore, he'd—"I'm there!" His eyes closed, white flashes interspersed with blasts of yellow, blue and teal moved through his field of vision and deeper into his psyche. His wolf howled thrice. Golden eyes blinked at him twice and disappeared. Logan inhaled slowly, pressing his lips together. Howls died in his throat. The time would come when he and his wolf would cry out their ecstasy together as their psyches united with Cassandra's in the ultimate commitment and dance of passion and fulfillment.

Cassandra moaned and rocked forward, placing her hands on Logan's shoulders. Shudders began deep within her, rapidly racing upwards and outwards as tsunami-sized waves of orgasmic energy swept over and through her. Logan's steady pressure on her clitoris redirected each orgasmic wave back along her vagina and deep into her G-spot. Throb and pulsate. Constrict and. . ."Oh goodness! Multiples!"

She rocked back and forth. Spasm after spasm pulsed up and down her inner being until her inner shield gave way. Reds and mauves greeted her inner sight. Yellows and blues bubbled and burst into flames that grew brighter until her vision cleared.

Logan smiled and nodded as his gaze met hers. He blew her a kiss and slid his hands up her arms. He embraced her, pulling down until their flesh once again touched, resting in each other's embrace as their psyches, physical bodies and minds slowed their orgasmic high and returned to their planes of being.

"Sweetie, rolling on our sides is going to make things a lot easier. You up to it." Logan rubbed his hands up and down Cassandra's back. Trying to copy the pressure she'd used on his calf earlier. The soothing strong strokes mixed with pressure. Letting her know he was here for her. Ready to TLC her as needed and make sure the condom didn't leak or come off before he and it were safely outside once more.

He knew and felt every breath Cassandra took. There was no way he couldn't laying flesh to flesh with her. Her heart beat close to his. One word came to mind with each beat of their hearts. The L word. One that Cassandra had used earlier then looked away when talking about being with loved ones. Were any of them ready to say the word allowed? Say it in a way that significantly changed their commitment and earlier declarations of being family together?

"I think so. Gotta get the condom off you." Cassandra tried to move.

Logan tightened his hold on her. "Move too quickly and chance of condom slipping off or breaking happens."

Cassandra let go a deep sigh. "How we do this? Don't need pregnancy complicating things."

Logan stroked his hands up and down Cassandra's shoulders twice. "I want children. Not without mutual agreement between my partners."

"Understood." Cassandra lifted her head, kissed his lips, and added, "I'm ready to roll on my side. Can you pull out holding on to the condom and you?"

Logan worked his hand between them. He clasped the base of his cock near his balls. "I'm going to inch my fingers up a bit. Try to hold still for a couple of moments."

Partway up his cock, his fingers touched the edge of the condom slicked with their joint orgasmic juices. He eased his fingers a bit higher, carefully wrapping them around the condom and himself. "Ease yourself off me bit by bit. No hurry. I've got a hold of the condom."

"I'm going to roll on my side carefully." Cassandra moved to her right, gliding off Logan. Part of him slipped out of her. "Still got a hold on things?"

"Yes. Got me and the condom."

"Are you ready to pull out?"

"I think I already am."

Cassandra reached between them. Her hand brushed Logan's slicked fingers and part of the condom. "I'm going to move away."

Quick slippery movements separated them. Logan looked down. His lips pressed together. Whatever the outcome, cursing loudly wasn't going to change the results.

"Condom's still on me. Taking it off now." Logan worked the condom up and off him. "Do we check now about leaks or wait?"

Cassandra rose, pulled on her nightgown. "Best way I know to check is run water in it."

Logan nodded. "Help me pull my briefs on. We'll find out together."

A few moments later, Logan, with Cassandra's help, quietly crutched into the bathroom. By the low glow of the nightlight, they quickly rinsed and dried each other's nether regions. Cassandra turned the faucet on until a slow stream flowed out. Logan clasped the open end of the condom between the fingers of both hands and thrust it under the stream. Water flowed in and. . .overflowed back out the top. Cassandra stuck her hand below the condom, wiggled her fingers and brought them back up staying clear of the water running down the condom and over Logan's fingers and hands.

She touched her face and lips. Turned to Logan doing the same to him.

Logan turned the condom over, emptying it. Tossed it in the toilet and flushed.

"Let's get some sleep." Logan placed both crutches under his arms. "No surprises to worry about."

"Yes. Our first mating and no surprises." Cassandra pressed her lips to Logan's and moved back. "We're ready to sleep. Worried-filled dreams aren't awaiting us."

Back in bed, they cuddled close to each other. Logan's arm around Cassandra's waist. Her hand resting on his. Covers over them as sleep drew them into its deep embrace.

Logan pulled the covers higher. Somewhere in the midst of the darkness enveloping the house, he'd awaken listening to the wind whistling through the trees outside the bedroom window. Ice pelts pinged as they hit the window before the wind died back down and silence once again flooded through the house. Getting back and forth to the bathroom without waking Cassandra had taken several moments. Dakota had waved as he and Dulce wandered back into the den, closing the door behind him. Logan pulled his bedroom door to, not clicking it shut, hoping Dulce didn't decide to make a bolt for his room. The scamp hadn't fussed. Logan whispered a thankful prayer as he washed and dried his hands. Back in bed, with Cassandra snuggled to him, Logan fell back into dream-filled slumber.

He squinted looking at the clock on the bedside table. *It was eight a.m.* When he got back in bed after using the bathroom, it was almost three a.m. He'd slept deeper, dreamed more, and was—relaxed. His ankle twinged some after he'd gotten back in bed. Warmth and knowing he'd gotten to and from the bathroom on the crutches by himself had soothed his inner angst. His wolf had curled up beside him, nuzzled his psychic hand and lulled him back into healing slumber. Logan stretched under the covers, reaching to his side, ready to snuggle closer to Cassandra. Cold air greeted him. He snatched his hand back. Where was Cassandra?

Cassandra hung her towel on the rack. She checked the clock as she entered her bedroom from her bathroom. Eight-fifteen. Logan was still asleep when she got up. Sleeping past daybreak was unusual for her. Given she and Logan hadn't fallen asleep until possibly after midnight, she was surprised she'd slept until sevenish.

Making her way out into the hall, she'd paused. Dakota's door was closed indicating he and Dulce still slept. Showering and using the bathroom had given her time to gather her thoughts. Time to weed through the blips, images and feelings that fueled her thoughts. Doubts fled from her subconscious taking with them her past lackluster self-perceptions she wasn't good enough. That measure crept its way out with the wind blowing past the house. Good enough was her perception. Her judgment call and her decision. She was good enough. Whatever came out of this time with Dakota and Logan, she'd gained a gift. An extraordinary gift. She had what it took to attract potential mates. Opening herself to the broader view and diverse acceptance of her world and the people in it. As she finished dressing and brushing her hair, her heart whispered its message. She smiled, nodding as she opened her bedroom door.

CHAPTER TWENTY-ONE

Dakota turned over, opened one eye and blinked. Sunlight danced across the floor, illuminating a path of patches growing in size until. . .he blinked again, opening both eyes. Daylight peeked in around the edges of the curtains covering the windows. Where the curtains didn't meet, light lit the patchwork path crisscrossing the floor and area rug right up to the side of the bed where its descent began. A jagged, misshaped circle danced close to where Dulce lay watching him.

He yawned and stretched. Sleep had enveloped him most of the night. The cool bathroom tiles against his bare feet as he emptied his bladder twice during the night reminded him he wasn't. Mad dash to the bathroom nude and hoping he didn't flash Cassandra or Logan filled his dream-laden sleep with laughs and odd dreams. Dreams that perhaps opened the door between his psyche and his wolf. Twice, his wolf appeared lying next to him as he sat on a tree stump overlooking a river. A river his wolf challenged him to ford across. On the opposite bank, two people sat with their backs to him. In the second dream, his wolf walked beside him as he entered the shallower part of the river where a rock path appeared. A golden light beamed down on the spot where he planned on exiting the river. The woman on the bank held out her hand to him. The male opposite her did the same. His wolf bounded up the bank and sat on its haunches between the two people. One word formed in his mind and pulsated with every beat of his heart. Home. He was home. His wolf howled twice and the vision cleared. Just as the vision cleared, the faces of the man and woman came into focus. Entwining hands, Logan and Cassandra welcomed him home.

Dakota sat up. The spiritual side of his supernatural half showed their blessings through his dreams. Could he, Logan, and Cassandra make the vision reality? He pulled on his briefs and opened the bedroom door. Logan's room door was open. Dulce jumped off the bed and ran across the hall into Logan's room. Dakota took a breath, held it, offered a short prayer of thanks and crossed the hall ready to knock on Logan's door. Dakota raised his hand.

Dulce ran out of the room and down the stairs barking.

"Dulce, what is it?" Cassandra called out. Sounded like she was in the kitchen.

"Dakota must be awake." Logan's next words were muffled.

Dakota turned back, ready to pull on his clothes and forego showering until later.

Thump. Muttered curse words followed. Another thump sounded.

Dakota stepped off the upstairs landing, ready to take action.

"Sorry if we woke you." Logan came into view. He crutched forward, wearing the supportive boot he'd gotten at the ER.

"You're okay?" Dakota moved down another step.

"Yeah. I called the ER doc's answering service. Wanted to know about wearing the boot." Logan rubbed his ass. "Wheeling around is okay. Numb ass isn't."

Cassandra moved up beside Logan. "Lovely view, Dakota."

Dakota looked down and back up. "Yeah, wash and wear pjs are in vogue."

Cassandra stepped up next to Dakota, slipped an arm around his waist and hugged him to her. "Your pjs are awesome. I hope you'll model them for me tonight after we shower together."

"I think I can arrange that. Don't step away too quickly."Dakota leaned into Cassandra's embrace, whispering. "I got a boner that won't behave."

Cassandra reached between them, cupped him with her hand and squeezed lightly. "I don't think Logan is going to ogle you."

Dakota snorted. "Probably not. No need to advertise where my nethers thoughts are."

Logan cleared his throat. "Dude, no need to hide it. Saw it already."

Dakota peered over Cassandra's shoulder. One eyebrow arched giving Logan a squinty-eyed look. "When's breakfast?"

Cassandra hugged him again, whispering in his ear. "You're not jealous, are you?"

Dakota turned, kissed Cassandra and leaned partly away from her. "No. Half awake. Need caffeine and food."

"And a shower?"

"That too." Dakota turned. His hard-on brushing against Cassandra. "Need some relief too. Be down in about ten minutes."

Dakota continued back up the stairs. Mornings weren't his thing. He'd slept deeper and harder than the prior night. Signal he was comfortable with the place, people and atmosphere. His trouble was not fully awake. His adrenaline dissipated as quick as it had leaped into action. He'd apologize after he showered and took care of his dang hard on. He'd bound up the stairs except bouncing in that state wasn't entirely pleasurable. Pain was not a pleasure inducement for him.

Cassandra made her way back down the stairs. She paused as she reached Logan. "Not much of a morning person."

Logan grinned and nodded. "To quote Dakota, one of his prize possessions is his programmable coffee maker. He usually finds his awake personality after halfway through his second mug."

"What happened yesterday morning?" Cassandra continued on into the kitchen.

"Adrenaline. He got caffeinated before the rush stopped. Don't sweat it. He's fine. We're fine." Logan leaned against the counter. "What we fixing for breakfast?"

"Pancakes and bacon." Cassandra set the coffee can on the counter. "Plus a full pot of this."

Logan chuckled. "I saw some orange juice in the freezer. Make that up and add a few of the dried blueberries to the pancakes. You'll have his sweet tooth satisfied and caffeinated at the same time."

"And you?" Cassandra placed the box of pancake mix and dried blueberries on the counter.

"I'm fine with a couple of swallows of coffee before I eat. I'm the morning person between Dakota and me. Running joke is see me first for any police stuff in Sylvan Valley and Dakota later in the day for Cauldron Falls things." Logan set two mugs on the counter next to the mixing bowl and carton of eggs.

"A night owl and a crowing rooster." Cassandra turned the coffee maker on. "You said you were *wolf* shifters. *Not birds.*"

Logan pressed his lips together, catching part of his upper lip between his teeth. A snicker sounded, followed by another. Mirth barreled up his throat, pushing hard and fast over his tongue, slamming into his teeth and lips barrier. He looked down, counting breaths and back up. Movement next to him caught his attention. Cassandra set a mug of coffee in front of him. He faced her.

Cassandra saluted him with her mug, licked her finger and drew five lines in the air. "Score."

Logan picked his mug up with two hands, blew on the coffee, and sipped. He'd hoped Dakota remembered to wake up his sense of humor. One ironical wit plus one satire wit plus one lousy joke teller equaled he didn't know what. Logan hoped by the time Dakota came down, he'd had enough coffee and practiced his delivery, he stood a chance of not missing out on too much of the conversation.

Dakota shut the bathroom door. He combed his fingers through his hair. Ten-minute shower. Standing in front of the mirror admiring himself didn't do much except remind him he needed to braid his hair after he washed it. May be he'd get Cassandra to do it. Debating how to start that conversation wasn't getting him soaped, jacked off and rinsed. He stepped into the tub, pulled the shower curtain closed and turned the faucet to warm. Ducking under the lukewarm spray, he worked the soap over his chest and arms. Over his ass cheeks and down his legs. Under the shower again, rinsing and standing still, letting the water run down him. Taking with it his uneasiness, lingering doubts and waking him up.

Self-doubt could be one hellish pain in the ass. He'd doubted himself not concerning Cassandra or Logan. Doubt came from where did things go from here. Law enforcement dealt with unknowns to a point. Clues, investigations and research combined together to reveal answers. Cauldron Falls had their pranksters, thieves and malicious idiots and the wanna-be who thought they were top dog in their family or pack. Yeah, letting a few stew in a cell for a couple of days usually got their vision cleared and understanding respect, diversity acceptance and it taking everyone coming together as a community.

Dakota soaped his hands, put the bar of soap down, and cupped his testicles. He ached from no release other than a quick orgasm when he woke in the night after a very vivid dream of him and Cassandra making love. The L word populated his dream narration frequently. He'd whispered it aloud as his first stroke slid and back down him, Second stroke a bit faster. Third same as the second. Each next stroke a bit faster. His hand tightening around him on the next upward fondle. One more back down and up. . .His balls swelled, his heart throbbed faster and. . .

"*Yes!*" he hissed, trying to keep his voice down. Deep inside him, the volcano smoked, pumping out blasts of hot air and spills of lava. The thunder and rumble shook him from inside out. One spurt of jism. Then another until semen coated his hands. He rocked back on his heels, panting as one last orgasmic burst ripped through him. Dakota leaned against the wall, gulping air through his mouth. Hot sweet short orgasms pushed him into awake. Intensity of this one had him teetering on telling Logan and Cassandra he was going back to sleep. Could he admit he'd jacked off?

Dakota soaped and rinsed again, working his soapy hands through his hair. Shampooing it would come later. He'd ask Cassandra to help him blow dry it. Frizz ran in his family. A few great-grands and several recent family additions had curly hair. His showed up at the dangest moments like blow-drying it. Nothing wrong with curls. Just a major pain braiding long curly hair insisting on frizzing. He shut off the shower and hung up his towel. Braiding his hair would take a few moments.

He glanced at the wall clock. Three minutes left to dress, braid and get down the stairs. Fashionably late never hurt. Damn straight, it didn't hurt. He wasn't leaping down any steps or sliding down banisters either like he did as a kid. A few well place splinters stopped that fast entrance career real quick. Dakota rubbed the spot where it took his mother and grandmother over fifteen minutes to extract all the splinters and apply first aid cream to his bum posterior.

He pulled on clean briefs and t-shirt. Sitting on the bed, he combed his fingers through his hair, separating it into three sections. He could braid in his sleep. The last time he full moon morphed, several of his pack mates chased him three miles baying all the way that he wasn't him. No long-haired tail. Took him four months to convince them his wolf didn't match his human hair. Dakota finished his braid, stood, and pulled his jeans and shirt on. A knock rattled the den's door as he pulled his socks and slippers on. "Come in."

Cassandra entered carrying a mug with steam rolling off it. She held the mug out to him. "Figured you could use this."

"Thanks." Dakota sipped the coffee. Hot, sweet and black. Cassandra remembered how he liked his coffee. "Suppose Logan said who's the morning person and who is late morning between us."

"Yeah, rooster and an owl." Cassandra sat on the bed. "Do you mind me asking a question?"

"No. Go ahead." Dakota sat next to her. He drank more of his coffee.

"Are you okay that Logan and I had..." She swallowed hard. Admitting she and Logan were intimate wasn't coming out like she rehearsed it all the way up the stairs.

Dakota set the mug on the nightstand. He took hold of her hand. "Am I okay you and Logan had sex?"

"Yes."

"No need to look away." Dakota turned, facing her more. "Envious. Some. Curious. For sure. Needing to know details? Not beyond did you enjoy yourself."

Cassandra rested her head on Dakota's shoulder, needing to touch him. Reassuring herself, she heard correctly. "Not jealous? Or wanting a threesome?"

Dakota let go of her hand. "Threesome?"

"Maggie said lots of threesomes happen in triads."

"Hon, don't mean I'm expecting it. Did Logan say he was?"

"We hadn't discussed it. Is this something we need to discuss together?."

Dakota put his hands on her cheeks, tipped her head back, and brushed his lips over hers. "Together is okay. Individually is good, too. I'm not into threesomes."

Cassandra let out a long, slow sigh. "Thank you."

"You're welcome. Never be afraid to ask. Pleasure is a mutual thing. Partners sensuality varies." Dakota picked up his mug, drank most of the cooled coffee and handed her the mug. "I'm famished. Let's go eat."

Cassandra walked to the den door. "Pancakes and bacon? Blueberry pancakes?"

Dakota rubbed his hands together. "Delicious. No short stacks. Six pancakes, please, with butter and syrup."

Cassandra followed Dakota out the door and down the stairs. Would their joint sexual intimacy discussion go easily for the three of them?

CHAPTER TWENTY-TWO

Logan saluted Cassandra and Dakota with a batter-covered whisk as they entered the kitchen. "Griddle is hot. Batter ready to spoon out. Blueberries rinsed, sugared and stirred. Want blueberries in or on top of your pancakes."

Dakota rubbed his hands together. "Either way is good. Coffee, sweet, and black. Pancakes and blueberries. Butter and syrup."

"Who's cooking the bacon?" Cassandra set a frying pan on the stove. "I've got pancake duty."

"Easy fast way is on a plate covered with paper towels three strips at a time." Dakota placed three plates on the counter. Covered them with paper towels. "I'll handle the bacon. One goes in as done one comes out."

Logan pushed back from the table. "I'll let Dulce in. Tied her leash to the screen door handle."

Cassandra looked at Dakota, shrugged and poured pancake batter on the griddle. "Aren't you overdoing it, Logan?"

"ER doc's service called while you were upstairs." Logan steadied himself with his crutches as he stood. "Less wheelchair. Move more if swelling down. Wear support boot when moving."

"Great news." Cassandra flipped the first batch of pancakes. "Sore arms?"

"Oh yeah. Hot packs. Massage." Logan winked at Cassandra. "Warm showers."

"Means one of us in there with you." Dakota set the bacon filled plate on the table. He put the syrup pitcher in the microwave to warm.

"I choose Cassandra." Logan leaned against the wall, opened the back door and let Dulce in. "Good girl. I can see you pooped and peed."

"I'll shovel the steps after breakfast." Dakota looked out the window. "Not much snow last night."

"I noticed a few flakes when I got up around four." Logan untied Dulce's leash from the screen door handle. "Still damn cold out."

Microwave chimed. Electric kettle whistled. Cassandra put a platter filled with pancakes on the table. Dakota poured coffee in his and Logan's mugs. Logan put utensils, sugar bowl and carton of half and half middle of the table.

Cassandra pulled out the chair closest to her. "Logan, sit please. You're hobbling some."

"Yeah, kinda stiff." Logan dropped into the chair. "Thanks, Dakota, for taking Dulce's coat off."

"All part of taking care of each other." Dakota set a mug of hot water and a tea bag in front of Cassandra. "Time to eat."

A few please and thanks mixed with pass the bacon and more pancakes while they ate. Cassandra pushed her almost clean plate away from her. Listening to the news and weather updates had distracted her thoughts. Dakota had turned off the radio before refilling his and Logan's mugs with coffee and her mug with hot water and a fresh tea bag. Her prior question kept returning. Pinging her with jabs and pokes. Part of it had to be the unknown. How to handle the situation calmly. How did she nonchalantly put the question out there? Was there any delicate way to introduce the topic? Was this one of those bare-it-all topics Maggie said she'd heard about?

Cassandra laid her spoon down next to her mug. It was now while none of them had mouthfuls of anything. "I have a question."

Logan set his mug back on the table. "Your tone says this is serious."

Dakota put his utensils down. "Is this about our discussion upstairs?"

Cassandra nodded. "Yeah. I need information. Is this new for you?"

Dakota speared a forkful of pancakes. "I know this is a fork. It's got pancakes on it. To someone else, they might be hotcakes or a word their family uses. Do I know how I want to go about this? Yes."

"I'm new to this too." Logan pointed to the bowl of sweetened blueberries sitting next to the syrup pitcher. "I know what went into that mix. I know I can eat it. Someone else may not make it the same way."

"Dakota, are you saying you aren't new to triadic relationships?" Cassandra pulled her plate to her. She broke her remaining piece of bacon in half, popped it in her mouth and chewed.

"No, I'm saying I know what we've been and are talking about. Us as a three-person family group. Others might call it triad. Some a particular designation call it a V." Dakota ate the pancakes.

Cassandra swallowed and turned, facing Logan more. "Okay, here is what I asked Dakota upstairs, Logan. Is he okay you and I had sex?"

Logan sputtered, quickly set his mug down and glanced at Dakota. Dakota nodded and kept eating. Logan gripped his mug handle firmer. He and Cassandra had sex. No doubts there. His description included the L word, making love. Euphemism aside, his heart was in those moments. His wolf bonded with Cassandra in those moments. His heart wasn't letting go of the L word description. Were they going to dance around semantics or did he come out and say, 'Cassandra, I love you'?

He uncurled his fingers from the mug handle little by little. Focusing on each move, he envisioned words to express his in the moment feelings. Curious. Uneasy. Unknown and why did she ask? More questions sprang up. Logan chose one word to focus on. Curious. His success with multipartner relationships was a few secondary friends with benefits. Good friends who were lovers. Friends who loved him and he them. Not the way his heart pinged every time he held Cassandra. Talked with her and even the flood of emotional tenderness and want to be with her again like they were last night. Sharing and mutually enjoying their physical and emotional intimacy.

"This must be important to you. Or you wouldn't have asked." Logan resumed eating.

Cassandra crumbled the rest of her last bacon strip on top of the remainder of her pancakes and syrup. She cut things into small pieces, speared some with her fork, and laid it on her plate. She glanced at Dakota. He stacked his empty plate on the serving platter along with the bacon plate and his utensils.

"I'm going to deflate the imaginary elephant in the room." Dakota placed his hand on hers as he spoke. "Do I care? Do I want to know? Yes to both. To the extent both of you enjoyed yourselves and there's nothing that put any of us at risk. We already talked about health matters."

"I'm new to this multi-partner relating." Cassandra added her plate to the growing stack middle of the table. "I've said this before. I'm saying this again. I don't want to lose either of you or your friendship. You're important to me."

Dakota set his mug right side up next to the stacked plates and utensils. "I'm not jealous or envious of either of you. Physical intimacy is part of our family. I'm compersive for you and Logan. I hope he'll be the same when you and I are intimate."

"Compersive?" Cassandra asked.

"Being compersive is sharing in the joy we bring each other. Your joy is my joy and vice versa." Dakota clasped Cassandra and Logan's hands. "I've learned to trust my gut and heart. My spiritual wolf guide appeared in my dreams."

Logan leaned forward. "Mine too. Dakota, what did yours show you?"

"Showed me the stepping stone path through the river to where two people sat holding hands." Dakota paused. "Before I share more, I want to hear Logan's dream."

Logan nodded. "Okay. My wolf curled up next to a sleeping woman. He barked as I got closer. He got up and nudged me closer until I stood tight to her. He laid down close to us. His eyes glowing. Two words came to mind. Mates and home."

Dakota turned his empty mug over. Doing the same with Logan's mug and Cassandra's. Trickles of coffee and tea ran out from beneath the mugs forming a small pool on the table. "We can hide under our fears and concerns. Or we can follow the path to our combined desire. Which is our united choice?"

Logan pulled his mug to him, turning it right side up. "Hiding increases fear. Concerns overtake our thoughts and fog our perception. I choose to move forward with you and Cassandra. Together united in building our dream of family."

Cassandra uprighted her mug. Picked it up and placed it in front of her. "I'm done with being alone. I still need space to decompress after work. I'm choosing to learn how to do that with you, Dakota and you, Logan at my sides. I chose building our dream. Our definition of family together."

Dakota grasped his mug between his hands. "My wolf led me to the light illuminating the river I needed to cross. The spot where I hadn't seen the shallow and rock path. On the opposite bank sat two people. A man and a woman. When the light shined on them, it was both of you welcoming me to the circle you started building. Home and family were the words I heard my wolf howl."

Cassandra pointed to the coffee-tea pool close to the middle of the table. "The trickles from each mug represent our input. Our finding our way to the bigger picture. Us as a triadic family?"

Dakota stood and picked up the stacked dishes. "Triad. Trifamily unit. Whatever designation we agree upon. Like getting ice cream at the multiflavored shop in town. Your combination might differ from someone else's. So can definitions."

"I'm not worried about defining." Logan wiped the coffee-tea pool up with paper towels. "What about our hearts? Emotional connection. How do you feel Cassandra, about the L word?"

"L word?" Cassandra glanced from Logan to Dakota.

"Depends on the L word Logan's talking about." Dakota smiled and shrugged. "I suspect he's talking about L-O-V-E."

Cassandra swallowed, pressed her lips together, and swallowed again. Why did her throat choose now to go dry? Why was Logan asking about love? They all said they cared about each other. Goddess, love took on many different meanings and interpretations. If that was where their conversation had evolved to, what was her answer? Could she say she loved Dakota and Logan? Loved them together? Or uniquely as each of them were?

She pressed her palms flat against the table. The woodgrain's coolness swept across her palms and disappeared as quickly. Warmth replaced the lingering chill. Cassandra picked up the sugar bowl, carton of half and half and walked to the sink. She set them on the sink counter and turned. Logan faced away from her, gathering the rest of the dishes and mugs. Dakota rinsed the dishes he cleared off the table and placed them in the dishwasher. Dulce sat close to her food dish taking in all they did. Her tail wagged from time to time. Mood, emphasis and calm could evaporate, change and morph at any moment, given word or nuance. Had they foraged across another river like Dakota had in his dream? Become family and mates within the limited amount of time they'd spent together?

"Logan, is Dakota correct? You're asking about the L-O-V-E word?" Cassandra put the half and half in the fridge. She turned back catching Logan and Dakota watching her.

"What if I am?" Logan dried his hands and hung the towel on the under-the-cabinet towel rack.

"Do we need specifics? This is the exact thing we're talking about?" Dakota filled Dulce's food dish and water bowl. He picked up his hikers and sat in the chair closest to him. "I'm not poopooing it. Asking what, if any, boundaries there are."

Dakota pulled on his hikers, tied them, and stood. "I'm going to think about what my definitions are, where my emotions and thoughts are at while I clean the steps."

"I'm gonna do the same while I tidy the living room." Logan crutched his way into the living room.

"Cassandra, busy work helps me think. Is there something you can do while Logan and I are choring?" Dakota zipped his parka and pulled on his watch cap.

"Probably gather a load of laundry. Mixed load with stuff from each of us." Cassandra started toward the kitchen door.

"Good. My part of the load is in my laundry basket." Dakota opened the door. "I'll be done in about fifteen minutes."

Cassandra paused as Dakota clicked the back door shut. Fifteen minutes to gather her thoughts. Fifteen minutes to decide what the bloody hades the L-O-V-E word meant to her. It was five years since she even considered putting words to the feeling much less telling someone the word other than her grandparents and a few cousins.

CHAPTER TWENTY-THREE

Dakota walked to the edge of the driveway. Sweeping snow off the steps took less time than cleaning up Dulce's potty run had. The sun peeked out from behind the clouds for a moment before the wind kicked up. Ice and bits of crusted snow danced in the air, swirled around him and continued their erratic boogie down the street and sidewalk. Two of the neighbors across the street waved as they cleared off their cars and walks. Mounds of snow marked the sides of driveway aprons. Several people were breaking the mounds down and tossing them in their front yards in an effort for their neighbors and themselves to move their vehicles. How like the conversation he, Cassandra and Logan were having. Breaking down the barrier mounds keeping them from moving into a trusted discourse. One key word for him right there—Trust.

Trust that everyone spoke their truth. Spoke from their heart and mind. Not all of what was said or would be guaranteed a successful outcome. More communication would happen. Part of life. Relationships evolved. People changed and no two moments in life were exactly the same.

He made his way back to the back steps and porch. Icicles hung off the railing. Bursts of mini rainbows scattered across the concrete. Momentary illusions if someone got caught in daydreaming instead of focusing. Not always easy to do. Dakota leaned against his truck. His second word easily came to mind. Commitment. Commitment to working together. Commitment to what they wanted. Not what others thought they should have or should be doing things their way.

He knew his third word as he opened the back door and glanced at the kitchen clock. Understanding. Time and space came right along with understanding. Each of them needed to understand themselves and each other. He required his remaining five to six minutes to sit with a mug of coffee and let his thoughts run rampant. He probably had a half dozen more words that he could toss out. Connecting everything together was going to take him a couple of moments quiet to accomplish.

Logan slumped down against the back of the couch. Fifteen minutes to come up with words, definitions and what the L word meant to him. How did he define it? Thumbing through a few of the magazines he'd straightened twice on the coffee table offered flashes of nudges. The last time he used the word to describe how he felt about someone, they'd beat feet in the opposite direction faster than he could finish what he was saying.

His friends with benefits lovers hugged him. Told him they cared. Even signed a few of their notes and cards with the L word. Their discussions had degrees of separation and tiers of hierarchy. Relationship anarchy didn't fit his way of thinking either. What did?

One word that stood out was compassion. Caring and concern mixed with it. Love had so many synonyms and lots of antonyms. Several of the latter he'd learned about shortly after the Great Reveal. Prejudice reared its ugly head wherever and whenever it tried and could. Logan leaned forward. One word connected all those together in a unique way. Perseverance. Determination to live life in a fashion that embraced diversity. Okay, so he had two outer words. What were his core words? Caring, compassion, and affection. Physical and emotional intimacy mattered a lot. Not just talking. Actions showing and backing up words. Actions sometimes spoke louder than words. There was one thing that left him wondering on a different tangent. Rumors abounded during Cassandra's granddad's tenure as mayor and city council leader. He could read auras and was a bit empathic.

Cassandra tossed her clothes into Dakota's laundry basket along with the towels from her bath and the hall bath. Logan's laundry lay on his bed. The place they'd had sex. *More than that and you know it.*

"Shut up psyche. No one asked you." Cassandra reached for the clothes.

You asked. I'm you and stop trying to fool yourself. Your heart did a couple pitter patters when Logan showed concern beyond words about being careful and protecting you from busting the condom.

Cassandra stuffed the last of Logan's clothes in the basket and hurried toward the hall.

Scared? Darlin', after the way Theo broke your heart, don't blame you. Damn cheater. Use 'em and leave 'em pain in the ass. Unsure and skeptical are your watchwords.

"Sure are. Do you blame me?" Cassandra stepped into the hall and looked over her shoulder, knowing that her doppelganger wasn't behind her making faces.

No blame or shame, sister. Dakota and Logan have shown you friendship, caring and a hell of a lot more concern. Stop fighting feelings and verbalize them. Keeping your foot in your mouth ain't worth the soggy shoe and sock. Besides, there's better-tasting things to lick and suck, if you know what I mean.

Cassandra clutched the basket tighter, glancing back toward Logan's room one more time. Closed her eyes, took a deep breath, and slowly exhaled. Discussions happened because people talked. This discussion topic was one she never considered having. Dakota and Logan topped her interest list. Maybe Maggie was right. She'd become too cautious. Too busy guarding her back and not giving people a chance to show their true colors. She opened her eyes and made her way down the stairs. Time for keeping fences down and actively listening focused on the ongoing conversation had come.

Logan stood up as she reached the bottom of the stairs. "Got your words?"

"Pretty much. Gotta put the laundry in." Cassandra entered the kitchen. Dakota looked up, saluted her with his mug of coffee and looked down. "Dakota, you okay?"

Dakota nodded. "Yeah, deciding how bad I got the munchies."

"Dude, last time you had the munchies this close to breakfast you were prepping for a court appearance." Logan sat in the chair opposite Dakota. "Don't think that's happening."

"No. Nervous habit. My mom used to say she could tell when I was focused and concentrating. I could go through a box of cereal, several slices of toast and ask when was breakfast ready." Dakota pushed back from the table. "Do either of you know what a Ven diagram is?"

"A group of overlapping circles." Logan pointed to the chair in between him and Dakota. "Overlaps where similar relations between two or more items."

Dakota tossed a pad on the table and a couple of pens. "Correct. We've each got three priority words about the L word. Describing L-O-V-E for each of us."

"The pad is to see where we overlap. Come together. Build a bridge. Found our way across the river, shallow spot and steppingstones aside." Cassandra walked to the laundry room. "Let me get the wash started. Logan there's a canister of oatmeal raisin chocolate chip cookies next to the box of tea bags. Now seems like a good time for them."

"I'll make the coffee and tea. Put out the sugar, half and half and napkins." Dakota walked over to Cassandra, leaned down and brushed his lips over hers. "Logan gets his kiss when you come back from laundry duty."

Logan chuckled. "Okay this time. Maybe next time, we both kiss her before laundry duty. Incentive to get it done and come back for more of the same."

"Now that offer, I'll need a few to contemplate." Cassandra dumped the clothes in the washer, added detergent and pushed the start button. She set the basket on top the dryer. She ran down her priority words again. Of those, she was sure. She wished her sweaty palms would stop. Her fear wasn't surrendering easily. Were Logan and Dakota uneasy about taking things to a new level? Going deeper with their hearts open and forded new paths in new territory together and individually?

Logan put the cookie canister on the table along with a plate of cheese, cold cuts, and crackers. The discussion could take time or be over in minutes. Either way, a snackish lunch would keep the hangries at bay. Keeping focused might matter. Logan put the cheese in the fridge. He pulled out the bottle at the back of the upper shelf. Homemade Sangria coming up.

Half the bottle of wine over ice mixed with apple slices, orange juice, lemon juice and zest. Dakota and he wouldn't get drunk. Shapeshifters sobered quickly especially when eating. Their oaths of office and civic duty kept both of them from more than the occasional glass of hard cider on their days off. Cassandra enjoyed a glass of wine from time to time. She'd introduced Dakota and him to wine-tasting events.

Logan placed the pitcher filled with ice and homemade sangria on the top shelf of the fridge. He added glasses, napkins and dessert plates to the table. He set two cans of his fave navy bean soup on the counter. If they needed more to eat, warming the soup with the bits of leftover bacon from breakfast along with dicing up the ham steak he found in the meat and cheese bin would make a hearty filling soup.

"I thought we were having tea and coffee. Looks like we're not." Dakota rinsed his mug and set it in the sink. "You planning on cooking?"

"Might be. Simple and easy. You know I got those recipes down." Logan held up one of the cans. "You complaining about my cooking? Besides made a bit of homemade sangria to go with the meal."

Dakota chuckled. "Ain't got food poisoning yet. Seriously, do you want to put that on now?"

Cassandra set a two-handled pot on the stove. "What all do you need?"

"Dice up the ham steak, add the leftover bacon bits, and maybe a bit of diced onion and celery. Nothing much. Depends on what you got for spices."

"Couple of dried-out garlic cloves, a wilted celery stalk and a couple of baby carrots. Salt, pepper and onion powder." Cassandra opened the soup cans. "Letting it simmer while we talk sounds good."

"Agreed." Dakota put the ham steak on the cutting board along with the bacon. "I'm going first with my words. Verbalize them and why. Once soup is on, we can write them down on the diagram and see where we overlap."

Logan dumbed the contents of cans into the pot and added water. "Great idea. We're busy together and learning from each other at the same time. I like that."

Cassandra put the garlic, baby carrots and celery stalk next to the cutting board. "I'm in. Go ahead Dakota."

"Okay. My first word is trust. Trusting each other sounds simple. When you're lowering your guard and being vulnerable, if you don't trust the people you're with. . .all hell could break loose." Dakota stirred the bacon bits and diced ham into the soup. "Second is understanding. Lots of questions are gonna come and go. Gotta be open to asking questions and answering them. Understanding each other allows communication to flow. I'll wait on number three."

Dakota sat down at the table. He tapped the glass in front of him. "Maybe some sangria after we're done with the first round."

Logan wiped off the cutting board. "I really need to sit and prop my ankle up. Been going without crutches some. Not a good idea."

"I can get them for you." Cassandra started toward the living room.

"Get them later. Come sit down." Logan patted the chair next to him.

Cassandra sat. "Logan, you next or me?"

"Go ahead, Cassandra." Logan began chopping and dicing the garlic and celery stalk.

"I'm a bit nervous. I'll explain why in the second round." Cassandra scooted her chair closer to the table. "My first word is appreciate. You can do for people and not get a word of thanks. Some people take and never give back. Someone I'm relating to needs to appreciate what we have and show that. Second word is loyalty. No talking behind backs and using people."

"In the pot, please. I appreciate your help." Logan pushed the cutting board to Cassandra. "My first word is compassion. I may not agree with what someone says or does. Connection isn't happening if compassion and efforts to understand each other aren't happening. Second word is affection. Touches, hugs, and kisses are nice. We need four or more hugs to get through a day."

Cassandra stirred the celery and garlic into the soup and turned the burner to simmer. "Dakota, are we ready for round three?"

CHAPTER TWENTY-FOUR

"Round three after we decide which one of the first two words are our foundation words." Dakota pulled the pad to him. "Those words go here in the center of the overlapping circles."

"Which one is the most important?" Cassandra sat next to him.

"Priority. Not necessarily most important." Dakota picked up the pen and wrote his word. "Priority will change from situation to situation. For me most often, it's understanding. Communication happens when we get each other."

"Yeah, it's what do you build on relating to each other be it friends or family or more." Logan tapped the center overlap. "Mine is compassion. Empathy or sympathy depends on the circumstances."

Cassandra held her hand out. "Pen please. I've got two that are very interrelated. Loyalty and devotion. Sometimes I use part of each when I'm deciding on who gets in my inner circle."

Dakota laid the pen in Cassandra's hand. "One of those hyphenated words. I understand bits and pieces make up what we decide. Empathic like reading auras or energy signatures."

Logan glanced at Dakota. He shrugged and pointed to the pad.

"Our foundational words are understanding, compassion, and loyalty mixed with devotion. I think we've got a good sense of where we've been and are continuing to build on." Dakota turned the pad to Cassandra. "Anything to add or subtract?"

"Just this." Cassandra drew a heart around their foundation words. "A bit lopsided. It does embrace where we're at."

Logan kissed Cassandra's cheek and hugged her. "Are you showing you're feeling the L word?"

"Not sure what I'd call it. I know you and Dakota are part of my inner circle. Probably the closest I've gotten to anyone in quite a bit." Cassandra brushed her lips over Logan's. "Dakota, what do you think?"

"I like it. Inclusive and allows us freedom to be ourselves." Dakota tapped the pad. "Where's our second words go?"

"How about labeling each circle? That way, we know which is us." Cassandra handed Dakota the pen.

"Middle circle is Cassandra. I'm on the right. Logan the left." Dakota printed each of their names on top of their corresponding circle.

"Do you and Logan overlap other than center of my circle?" Cassandra asked.

"We form a bigger circle when we join hands." Dakota walked around the table and held out his hand. "Cassandra, take mine and Logan's hands. Logan and I join hands to complete the bigger circle."

"The unseen circle since we're talking about our inner overlap." Logan clasped Dakota and Cassandra's hands.

"The aura our circle pulsates is amazing. Yellows, reds, and ripples of energy." Cassandra squeezed Logan's hand. "Zoom. I send a ripple to you, Logan."

"I didn't think you saw it. Or felt it. We create aura-colored energy pulses." Reds and yellows streaked along their arms flowing toward Logan, pooling around his heart and upper arms. Logan looked at Dakota. "Zoom. I send a ripple out to you, my best friend."

" Zoom. I catch it and send it on to you, Cassandra." Dakota squeezed both Logan and Cassandra's hands.

Bands of golds, yellows, mauves and reds pulsed over and between them several times. Dakota let go of Logan and Cassandra's hands simultaneously. "I draw within me, deep into my heart, psyche and blending with my wolf spirit the friendship and caring that flows over me now."

"I do the same." Logan held his hands out, closing them and placing both over his heart.

Cassandra faced Logan and Dakota. "I take in your friendship and caring energy. Renewing mine and reigniting my belief in honest, ethical non-monogamous relationships."

Dakota hugged Cassandra and Logan as he made his way back to his chair. "Cassandra, what you just said makes me wonder have you tried non-monogamy before?"

"No, I'm new to doing it. Talked with Maggie and others who are non-monogamous. A dude named Theo swore he was interested in it, too. Screwed me over and not in a good way." Cassandra pulled the pad to her as she sat down. She wrote in capital letters appreciate close to her foundation word.

"That is why my second word is appreciate. Theo didn't try to understand me or talk about values."

"I'm sorry that happened. I hate when people abuse another person's trust and vulnerability. Theo did that big time." Logan clasped Cassandra's hand. He took the pen in his other hand and wrote his second word around the edges of where their circles intersected. "Your second word goes along with mine caring. Valuing someone includes being sensitive to their needs and core beliefs. You want to be helpful and accepting."

"That leads to my second word, trust. Trust is core to building relationships and friendships." Dakota wrote trust along the edge of the intersection of the circles. "Ready for our third words?"

Logan lowered his leg. "I need to stand up. Cassandra, could you get my crutches please. They're in the dining room."

"Sure." Cassandra hurried into the dining room.

Logan motioned Dakota closer. "When do we tell her we love her?"

"Soon. The words we're using are ones that define love. Even the ones Cassandra's using." Dakota helped Logan stand as Cassandra entered the kitchen.

"Here you go, Logan." Cassandra positioned one crutch under each arm. "Don't overdo."

"Thanks." Logan crutched over to the counter and leaned on it. "Numb ass ain't no fun."

Dakota snorted. "Numb other parts aren't either."

"No they aren't. They're getting a rest tonight." Logan grinned and winked. "I'm giving Cassandra the night off. Maybe she'll want to sleep with you."

"I might choose Dulce instead. I make my choice." Cassandra picked up the pen and pulled the pad to her. "My third word is respect. Respecting personal decisions, boundaries and preferences. Not that I'm disregarding an offer from either of you."

Dakota dropped into his chair, shaking his head and laughing. "She got us good."

Logan made his way back to his chair and sat down. "She did. Where do you want respect written, Cassandra?"

"How about right across the middle of all the circles? We need to respect each other." Cassandra hugged Logan and sat in her chair. "Across the lower portions of the circles is fine."

"I'll add my third word. Commitment. Keeping your word is important. Trust is built on that and the other words we've got."

"Sure does. My third word is affection. I like hugs and kisses. It's nice, too, to get a text that says thinking about you. A card or even email. Sometimes, it's taking time to make a meal and give space. It can take on different activities and/or words."

Dakota laid the pen down. "You know we've built a concrete idea out of our words. They're important to each of us. Think about it for a moment. Aren't we already doing this? Have been doing it?"

"We sure are. Respecting, devoted and committed to our friendship. Trust each other or we wouldn't be here. Compassionate and caring." Logan glanced at Cassandra. "What do you think, Cassandra?"

"Someone once told me that L-O-V-E was a noun and a verb. You did it. Said it in many different translations." Cassandra looped her arms around Logan's waist and hugged him tightly. "We're showing each other through words and actions the L word is part of us."

Cassandra moved closer to Dakota and motioned for him to stand. "I owe you a hug and a kiss. Not the friendly out-in-public ones. One that lets you know what I am thinking right now."

Dakota slid his arms around Cassandra's waist, pulling her tighter to him. He leaned down and whispered in her ear. "Seeing if you can get a reaction?"

"Could be. The one I got earlier today is worth replicating, don't you think?"

"How about we give it an official try later? I could use help with washing and braiding my hair while Logan finishes making the soup." Dakota pressed his lips to Cassandra's. Lips opened, tongues commenced a mating ritual that left no doubt of where their thoughts and actions could go. Dakota broke off the kiss and stepped back.

"Wow. That was scalding." Cassandra fanned herself. "We got lunch to eat. Wine to drink and soup to enjoy."

"Wine better with supper? I think you have all the ingredients for making crock pot roast." Dakota picked up the pad and pen. "Small pork roast will take about four hours. Need some of the wine and can use the left over chicken broth. A couple of sweet potatoes cubed. Can of peas and carrots. Spices rubbed into the scored roast."

"Sound delish. Almost a pork stew. I can make oatmeal bread to go with it." Logan rubbed his hands together. "Cassandra, all you gotta do is sit back and enjoy the catering."

"Not quite sit back. I need help braiding my hair after I wash it." Dakota filled the glasses with water. "I saw some board games in the dining room credenza. How about Chinese checkers while we lunch?"

"Loser washes dishes? Winner dries and set the table for dinner?" Logan tried to rise.

"Didn't know you two were competitive types." Cassandra stirred and tasted the soup. "Yup, almost ready. About ten minutes more."

"Board game tournaments and snowed-in were two watchwords in my family. Mini tournaments with the different games we had if family and friends were over." Dakota placed bowls on the counter and soup spoons and napkins on the table.

"I'll get the game board and accessories. Logan, check the soup please and see if it needs any last-minute seasoning." Cassandra exited the kitchen.

Dakota helped Logan position his crutches. "You up for gaming?"

"Sure am. My family loved Monopoly. Split up the properties and cash at start of the game. Every time you landed on someone's property you paid the bank. Whoever had the most loaned on properties won." Logan sampled the soup. "No other spices needed. Just a bit more simmering."

"Made up your own rules and game?" Dakota chuckled. "Musta made some pretty lively games."

"Sure did." Logan filled a food storage bag with ice and closed it. "Right now, it's how long can I stand the ice until pain pill kicks in time."

Dakota helped Logan prop his foot up and placed the ice bag on it. "Ten minutes then off. I'll be back in a moment."

Dakota met Cassandra at the kitchen doorway. "Gotta get the shampoo and my brush. Be back down in a moment."

"Logan and I'll set up the game." Cassandra entered the kitchen and stopped next to Logan. "Over did it? Need meds?"

"Yeah. Too soon for boot only. Take meds with lunch." Logan reached for the box Cassandra placed on the table. "Remember what compersive is?"

"Feeling joyful for your partners or friends about their joy." Cassandra set the box on the counter. "Why?"

"When Dakota kissed you, I felt the heat and the joy it brought both of you." Logan held his hand out. "I enjoy being compersive. Sharing joy is a great thing. Enjoying someone's joy multiplies in lots of ways. Make sense?"

"Yeah. Having a word that describes people's shared joy is nice. I've been with compersive coworkers, friends and relatives. Enjoying them experiencing or sharing their joy. Must have been what I felt in a different way seeing you and Dakota helping each other or kidding each other."

"I'm compersive seeing you and Logan talking like this." Dakota laid his brush, a towel and bottle of shampoo on the kitchen counter. "Seeing my partners enjoying each other brings me joy. All of us experiencing joy together brings me joy."

"No fair sneaking up on us." Cassandra poked Dakota's chest with her finger. "Since I'm being compersive, I'll share my joy in helping you brush out your hair before and after washing it."

Logan chuckled. "I think she's on to you."

"Ah could be." Dakota patted Logan's shoulder, hugged Cassandra and walked over to the stove. He lifted the soup pot lid, sniffed and grinned. "Time to eat, beat both of you at Chinese checkers, and let the dishwasher wash and dry the dishes."

CHAPTER TWENTY-FIVE

Dakota rinsed the suds off his hands, handed the last dish to Logan and faced Cassandra. "Winner was supposed to wash."

"You bet me one more game. We'd both won three games. Logan ceded he was drying." Cassandra blew Dakota a kiss. "Besides, you look so tempting wearing my apron."

Logan snorted and pointed to the one he wore. "Better than the ones my mom insisted we wear as kids doing dishes. Slogan suits me well. Kiss the cook, cleaner and dishwasher. You got the second load from your dinner prep."

Dakota dried his hand, hung the damp towel up and untied his apron. "Yeah, you didn't get the pink frilly one that says kiss the cook. Which you both did. And one of you is a much better kisser than the other. It ain't you, buddy."

Cassandra clapped her hand over her mouth. Peels of laughter escaped. Dakota pulled his apron off and tossed it at Cassandra. "You had to sneak Logan the red lipstick. Took me two washes to get it off my cheek. Come here, honey. I got something for you."

Dakota puckered his lips, reaching for Cassandra. She backed away, shaking her head. More laughter sounded. "Your lips are too red. Logan, you gave him my lipstick."

"Hey, why not?" Logan stood, steadying himself with his crutches. He held up the lipstick. "Dakota, can I join in?"

"Sure! Paint your lips. Both of us kissing all the available spots. Yeah, let's do it." Dakota matched Cassandra's sidestep, blocking her forward progression.

"Back toward me to the left," Logan called out. He pulled a chair closer to him.

"No fair blocking my escape." Cassandra dodged right. Logan shoved the chair at her.

"Depends on blocking. Escaping? No. Not happening. Two prong surround and kiss you? Oh yeah. Come on Dakota. You got her now." Logan grinned and crutched forward.

Cassandra turned around, ready to bolt. Dakota stood toe to toe with her. "Got ya. You gonna get pay back now."

Dakota wrapped his arms around Cassandra's shoulders and leaned down, capturing her ear lobe between his lips. He suckled and nibbled her ear lobe and let go. "One kiss down. Nice red earlobe. Logan your turn."

Cassandra scrunched her shoulders. "Don't suppose I could convince either of you to skip this and say you did it?"

"Oh darlin', you've got to be kidding. Miss nibbling your neck and leaving evidence I kissed you there? Nope, not happening." Logan's breath warned her neck and earlobe.

Cassandra tried to swallow. Her throat constricted as Dakota's and Logan's breath flowed over her exposed neck and down across her shoulders, dipping into the v-neck of her top. Logan slowly slid his hand up and down the curve of her hip, cupping her ass cheek and back to her hip. Dakota's palm body-hugged her midriff. Heat seeped through her top, trickling and pooling in and around her navel, soaking deep into her inner core. Dakota's other hand rested below her breast. His palm supported its fullness as his thumb moved back and forth tracing the undercurve.

Logan caught the underside of her ear between his lips suckling and laving. Goosebumps swelled, threading their way down her neck, settling within the heat pooling between her breasts. "Nips and nibbles. Marking you. Blending auras with you."

Lips captured flesh on each side of her neck. Worrying flesh with their lips and teeth. She was sure hickies and sucker bites adorned her neck and parts of her exposed collarbone area.

Dakota swept his hand lower, trailing heat down from her waist and inner female core, stopping short of the apex of her mons. Tidal groundswells washed down over her mons, nestling their way between her legs. Heat swamped her from her neck down to her labia and mons. Much more and she'd—"*Oh! Yes!*"

Cassandra clutched Dakota and Logan's arms. Orgasmic waves pushed their way up out of her, radiating surges and pulses unlike any she'd experienced before. Two men... both of them focused on her. Her pleasure and theirs mixed together. One last orgasmic blast pounded through and over her, tossing her up into an out-of-body experience. Blues, greens, reds and yellows mixed before her eyes. Dual wolves watched her. They sniffed the air and howled their joyous gratification at seeing and being part of her satisfaction. Shared gratification for the three of them.

Dakota wrapped his arm around Cassandra's waist, holding her upright. "You okay? Wanna sit down?"

"I think so." Cassandra inhaled and exhaled several times. She sat down with Dakota's help. She reached for Logan. "Logan, how you doing?"

"Awesome. Might not need that pain pill." Logan sat in the chair close to him. He grasped Cassandra's hand and let go.

"Three way make out sessions are fun." Dakota sat next to Cassandra. "Right three people and the generated energy pulses through everyone."

"For sure." Cassandra pinched part of her top between her fingers and worked it up and down. "I'll own it. You both got me off. I don't think I'll be able to wear that lipstick without shivers and pulses."

Logan licked one finger and drew five lines in the air. Grinned and pointed to Dakota. Dakota copied Logan's move. Both blew Cassandra a kiss.

Dakota placed his brush on the table, sat in his chair with his back to Cassandra, and undid his braid tie. "Cool downtime. Help me brush out my hair?"

"Distraction works. Refocus my thoughts and energy." Cassandra worked Dakota's braid apart strand by stand until his hair spread across his shoulders. Combing her fingers through the strands, she noted where the snarls were and worked them clear. She separated Dakota's hair into sections, working the brush down and across each section twice. Sensuality sizzled across her psyche and around her still partially aroused nipples, labia and clitoris.

"Thanks for that." Dakota pulled his chair over to the sink, turned the chair around, sat in it, and draped the towel around his shoulders. "Love a good scalp massage when I get my hair washed."

Cassandra turned on hot and cold water, tested the temperature and splashed a bit on Dakota. "Warm enough for you?"

Dakota wiped off his face. "My hair needs washing. You can do the rest of me later when we're alone. Your walk-in shower. You, me and lots of water and soap."

"Alone?" Cassandra wet Dakota's hair using the sink spray nozzle.

"Yes. Inviting you to spend the night cuddling with me." Dakota added as Cassandra lathered the shampoo into his hair, "Your bed since mine is small. More room for creative snuggling and cuddling."

Cassandra rinsed Dakota's hair, knowing his declarative invitation was the tip of what he had in mind. She knew from their earlier discussion the invitation was for him and her only. Dakota's tone and look said they'd need at least one or two condoms before they slept tonight.

"All done." Cassandra turned off the water and leaned down close to Dakota. She whispered in his ear. "Are you sure you got the stamina to keep up with my creativity?"

Dakota chortled. He sat up, pulling the towel off his shoulders and began towel-drying his hair. "We'll just have to see what happens."

"Okay you two. Dulce and I don't need to blush more." Logan lifted the crock pot lid and sniffed. His stomach growled. "Dakota, you got this recipe down."

"Thanks. No tasting before it's done." Dakota tossed the wet towel at Logan. "Check on the dryer. Load might be done."

"Come on Dulce. We're being told skedaddle." Logan crutched into the laundry room. Dulce hot on his heels.

"The storm outside is done." Dakota closed the space between him and Cassandra. He touched her heart, slid his fingers between her breasts, and down close to her mons. "Doesn't mean we aren't brewing our own in here."

Cassandra rubbed her lips together and voiced the one-word reply that occurred to her. "Okay."

A loud thump sounded. Logan's muttered cussing followed. Dulce forced her way out of the partially open laundry room door, scampering toward the living room.

"Logan, are you all right?" Cassandra asked, hurrying toward the laundry room. Dakota right behind her.

Yes. Laid one crutch on the washer. Didn't plan on Dulce insisting on getting between me, the dryer and my remaining crutch." Logan pulled the door open, hopping on one leg and leaning against the door jam. "Stubbed my toe, knocked my crutch out from under my arm, and it hit the dryer. Is Dulce okay?"

"Think so. She hightailed it into the living room. I'll check on her in a moment." Dakota shoved a chair close to the laundry room door. "Sit while Cassandra and I get your crutches and the dryer emptied."

Logan hopped to the chair and dropped into it. "Sorry. Wasn't trying to stir up chaos."

"You're fine." Dakota set the basket of clothes on Logan's lap. "It could have been Cassandra or me needing help. It's all good."

"What Dakota said." Cassandra handed Logan his crutches. "We can fold the laundry in the dining room. More room and Dulce probably staked out the couch."

Dakota dumped the basket on the dining room table. He pulled out chairs and sat in one of them. Cassandra in the one next to him. Logan in the one next to her. "Everyone grab a third and start folding. Don't matter who's it is. Make a pile for whose belongs to who."

Logan pulled several items to him. "Got a question about our earlier discussion."

Dakota pushed half of the remaining items to Cassandra and the last items to him. "What's your question?"

"Being thinking about the words we used. How they're common and what connects them." Logan laid Cassandra's folded bra and panties in front of him. "Aren't we talking about love? The L word and what it means to us."

Put socks in the middle. We'll pair them up separately." Cassandra tossed two socks in the middle of the table. "Kinda like playing poker except it words that we're playing with."

"I agree." Dakota tossed three socks in the middle. "I raise you one sock, Cassandra. The words you chose were words you use to define love?"

"I'm in as they say." Cassandra grabbed a sock out of Logan's pile, tossing it on the pile. "After the Theo debacle, I steered clear of emotional relationships beyond friends. Doing the Ven diagram helped me see where overlaps and comfort can happen. I'd say I'm emotionally connected to both of you. Possibly the L word, too."

"One thing I've learned from different relationships and pair bondings I know love varies from person to person." Dakota pushed his pile of folded clothes toward the center of the table. "Out of socks. Other clothes added. I love Logan like a brother, a chum and best friend. Cassandra, I love you. You've got a large chunk of my heart like Logan does."

"Look like I got all of 'em that you didn't!" Logan tossed five socks on the sock pile. "I'm gonna say it. Put it on the table. No more elephants. Cassandra, I love you. Probably have for some time. More than friends. I claim you as a mate and family triad member."

Dakota put his last two folded pieces on top of his others. "I'm baring my heart and soul here. Cassandra, I've wanted to claim you for some time. You make my heart sing. My soul happy and my wolf at peace. I'm claiming you as my triad mate and family member."

Cassandra pushed all the folded clothes aside and put the empty basket middle of the table. She picked up Logan's folded pile. "Logan, this basket represents home. A place where we can be ourselves. I add your presence here."

She put Logan's pile on one side of the basket. She faced Dakota. "Dakota, naming and claiming are parts of tonight's words and laying bare our hearts, intents and claiming them."

"Correct."

. "Each of you fills a part of my heart that others left cold and empty. Logan physically claimed his part last night. This evening he claimed the emotional part." Cassandra picked up Dakota's pile and placed it in the basket next to Logan's. "Right now, you claimed your emotional part of my heart. Tonight, you physically claim your part."

Cassandra picked up her pile plus the assorted socks. She held them over the basket. "This is my declaration. I claim my heart parts of you. Physically and emotionally. Tonight I will complete the physical with Dakota. Thank you, Logan, for last night."

She laid her pile across Dakota's and Logan's piles, strewing the socks over the top of the combined piles. "We folded each other's clothes and embraced our hearts and emotions. Dakota and Logan, I love you. I claim and choose you both as my triad and family mates."

EPILOGUE

Six Months Later

Cassandra laid the new book of short stories on the bedside table. Nightly cuddles with Dakota, Logan and her in bed reading stories to each other had become a regular event. Logan had hugged her and Dakota good night before scooping Dulce up and heading to his room.

Dakota got into bed next to her, cuddling close. "Jail's new HVAC system is working great. Air conditioning blasting. Furnace ready for the winter. Glad the city council agreed to the updates."

"Me too. Glad they decided to renovate and expand your office now that you've got more staff." Cassandra turned on her side, holding her hand out, palm up.

Dakota smiled. "Eager, are you?"

"Last night Logan and I celebrated our six-month marking anniversary. Tonight is our celebration." Cassandra laid the condom packet on Dakota's chest. She traced her hand down Dakota's chest, moving lower until she clasped his cock.

"Darlin', last time we tasted each other. Had a quick release and fell asleep." Dakota slipped his hand between Cassandra's legs. He slicked his fingers with her wetness. "Tonight, I want you on your hands and knees. I want to pleasure you two ways at once. Stroke your clit as I thrust in and out of you."

Cassandra jerked as he told her the position he wanted. Dakota learned about her sweet spots internally and externally the first couple of times they'd made love. Sex was replaced with lovemaking. Even Logan used the word. All of them used the L word easily with each other. Taking time and making time for joint pleasure topped their priority list.

Cassandra stroked upward until she reached his cockhead. She squeezed lightly and ran her fingers around his glans. She lifted her fingers to her lips and licked them. "You taste good. Every time I taste you or Logan, it's a wonderful treat. We're sharing a very intimate part of ourselves with each other."

"We're sharing all of ourselves with each other in many ways. The energy connection Logan and I share when we morph and run together in our wolf form is akin to energy mating rituals as two hetero-shapeshifter males get. That energy exchange is a bond I gladly share with Logan and he me. The mental and emotional intimacy we share with you is an awesome gift. Thank you for the gift." Dakota suckled each of his slicked fingers and lowered his hand.

Cassandra tore open the condom packet and took the condom out between her thumb and middle finger. She clasped Dakota firmly near his balls with her other hand. "Thank you for protecting me. We've all tested clean again. Birth control isn't optional until we know whether our biology will allow us to have children. Healthy children."

She worked the condom down and over Dakota's cock until the condom and her fingers reached where she held him. Their xenobiology tests turned out genomes that discovered Cassandra's latent aura reading and empathic magical genes. A lot of questions. Some still needing answers. Answers her grandparents and parents would provide during their visit next month. "Middle of the bed or where for this lustful delicious joining?"

Dakota rolled to the end of the bed and stood. He patted the area in front of him. "Right here. Easy simple access."

He watched Cassandra get on her hands and knees and work her way back toward him. Her breasts jiggled. Her pert ass cheeks jiggled. She moved without hesitation. He loved that he and Logan had helped ignite her confidence and self-esteem. Cassandra had moved into her own being. She valued herself, he and Logan and what they each brought to the triad. "A bit more."

Dakota moved between Cassandra's legs, resting one hand on her hip. He grasped his cock and slowly thrust forward, working his way deep into the heat he loved to feel squeezing him, holding him and welcoming him. His groin touched Cassandra's ass and mons. He wet two fingers and leaned forward, reaching between Cassandra's legs.

"Dakota," Cassandra moaned. "You're inside me. I love how deep you get this way."

"Me too." Dakota stroked over her clit in counter rhythm to his first thrust. Short quick thrusts. Quick strokes across her clit. Dakota applied pressure on his successive two strokes.

Cassandra countered her movements to Dakota's. He grasped her hips with both hands, pumping in and out faster. Out he pulled. She thrust back. It was as if they were of one body. One energy way spiraling them higher and hotter with each movement.

Dakota clutched Cassandra's hips tighter. So close. Not quite ready to spurt. One more—"*Oh lupa! I'm there!*" He slid his hand between Cassandra's legs, wet his middle and index fingers, and started stroking in rapid circles around and over her clit.

Cassandra tightened around him, arched her back, and moaned. "*Oh yes! Multiples!*"

Colors sparked around them. Reds, mauves, yellows and a kaleidoscope of colors enveloped them and dispersed. Dakota carefully wrapped his fingers around his shaft and the condom as he eased his way out of Cassandra. He took two steps and flopped down on the bed beside her.

Several moments passed while they returned to their physical bodies and caught their breath. Dakota helped Cassandra to her feet. They made their way to the bathroom holding hands. After a quick wash and rinse shower, they crawled back into the bed as a knock sounded on the bedroom door.

Logan opened the door. "Kinda lonely tonight. Not sure why. Mind if we sleep together?"

"Nights as a couple are great. I enjoy them." Cassandra got into bed and moved to the middle. "We've spent quite a few nights cuddled sleeping together. The bed feels empty without both of you beside me."

Dakota patted one side of the bed. "Here or over there. Make your pick."

Logan made his way around the bed and got in. "Thanks. By the way, Dulce snores."

Dakota snickered. "You just figure that out?"

Cassandra shook a finger at them. "We probably snore according to her."

Logan laughed and cuddled close to Cassandra. Dakota got in on Cassandra's other side, snuggling close as he pulled the covers over them. He reached for the light when a yip sounded. Dulce nuzzled his hand.

"Got room for one more?" Dakota asked, picking Dulce up and placing her at the foot of the bed.

Cassandra turned on her side, snuggling close to Logan and Dakota. "Where there are three loving hearts entwined, love abounds."

Don't miss out!

Visit the website below and you can sign up to receive emails whenever Solara Gordon publishes a new book. There's no charge and no obligation.

https://books2read.com/r/B-A-RAUJ-EJSOD

BOOKS 2 READ

Connecting independent readers to independent writers.

Did you love *Three Hearts Entwined*? Then you should read *Home for the Holidays*[1] by Solara Gordon!

Life changes are supposed to be exhilarating and fun, right? Elana Jones' retirement plans didn't include sharing a bed with the ex she'd given up catching a decade ago. Nor did her retirement plans entail reigniting a passion so heady and strong that she'd drop her old demeanor and embrace her sexy older self.

James Warren knows he's got another chance to grab Elana's attention and rekindle the flame of their past passion. How lucky can one shape shifter get when his holiday homecoming turns into a shared bed--forced proximity--that explodes into a passion that isn't stopping just because they're home for the holidays?

Read more at https://solaragordon.com/.

Also by Solara Gordon

Cascade Bay
Love Reborn
Reunited By Choice
Love's Triple Play
Three Hearts In Love
For the Love of Three

Cauldron Falls
Believe In Love
Home for the Holidays
Three Hearts Entwined
A Christmas Reunion

Peyton Corners
Falling for You
Caught by Love's Slow Burn

Standalone
A Heart's Desire
To Love You Again
To Love You Again

Watch for more at https://solaragordon.com/.

About the Author

Solara loves and lives with her partner of 21 years in the Metro DC area. What started out as a bi-coastal romance soon settled on one coast.

A vivid imagination keeps her busy creating her next fascinating romance. She enjoys creating unique characters and watching their journeys unfold. "Love freely given multiplies and will return endlessly" is a key aspect of her stories. Add in alternative lifestyles and her love for the paranormal, and the uncommon becomes the norm in many of her stories.

Her day job in the financial services industry pays the bills while she pens her erotic tales.

Read more at https://solaragordon.com/.